KATE H[

D. E. Stevenson's novel *Kate Hardy* is certainly one of her best. The story centres round The Dower House, an old house in a quiet English village. It is sold to Kate Hardy. She has never lived in a village before and finds her new neighbours interesting but difficult to understand. Kate is a very human person, humorous, sympathetic—and impulsive. She finds herself caught up in the life of the village, in the midst of strange happenings. The squire, who is the last of a long line of English squires, is a most unusual personality. There is a village carpenter who is a square peg in a round hole. There is an old Scotswoman with a forthright way of expressing her opinions. There is an old lady who claims that her ugliness gives her the right to pry into the affairs of her neighbours. The canvas is wide and colourful and the writing flows along in the beguiling manner we expect from D. E. Stevenson.

KATE HARDY

D. E. STEVENSON

COLLINS
8 Grafton Street, London W1
1990

William Collins Sons and Co. Ltd
London · Glasgow · Sydney · Auckland
Toronto · Johannesburg

ISBN 0 00 221993 X
First published 1947
This reprint 1990
Copyright D. E. Stevenson 1947

Printed and bound in Great Britain by
Billings Bookplan, Worcester

" Worth makes the man, and want of it the fellow :
The rest is all but leather or prunella."

POPE.

Part One

CHAPTER I

THE VILLAGE of Old Quinings started its existence as a huddle of cottages attached to a Priory which was famed throughout the district for its orchard ; and it was a moot point whether the village had derived its name from a particularly succulent species of pear or the pear had been named after the village. The Priory was now a ruin in the grounds of the Morven estate, but the orchard was still flourishing and still produced apples and pears in profusion. There was a parable here—or so the Vicar thought—for the strong thick walls of the Priory had fallen and were crumbling to dust, whereas the trees were alive and beautiful. They were not actually the same trees, of course, but descendants of those which the monks had planted. The stone thing had perished and the living thing was still alive—time had failed to destroy it.

Time had failed to destroy the orchard ; it had grown and flourished, so also had the Morven family, which had come to Old Quinings and settled here when the monks were dispossessed of their lands by Henry VIII. The present Richard Morven was directly descended from the first Richard Morven ; between the two Richards, linking them together, was an unbroken chain of Richards and Henrys whose portraits hung upon the walls of the Manor and whose bones lay in the family vault. The present Manor House was built in the reign of Queen Anne (replacing an older structure which had been destroyed by fire) ; it was of red brick, mellowed to a soft pink, delightful to behold. It stood upon a slight rise surrounded by fine old trees, and was approached by avenues from the south and west.

The village was charming. It had grown extensively

during the early years of the eighteenth century (the inn and coaching establishment at one end of the village street, the church, the hall and several very pleasant family residences in the neighbourhood all dated from that period and, like the Manor, were of red brick) ; after that period Old Quinings grew very slowly and presently stopped growing altogether, for there were no factories to bring people to the place : it was too far from London for business men to live and the railway service was deplorable.

Old Quinings did not mind being left behind in the march of progress ; it was quite pleased with itself. If people wanted factories and cinemas and a good railway service they could go elsewhere ; if they liked peace and quiet they could live at Old Quinings. It was just the right size—so its inhabitants thought—for it was large enough to provide all the amenities of civilised life and small enough to be a complete whole. Every one knew every one else and every one else's business.

The rumour that Mr. Morven had sold the Dower House was every one's business. There was not a creature in Old Quinings who was not interested in the news. Nobody had any idea how the rumour originated, but there it was, flying from house to house like a raging fire. The villagers heard it first, of course, but by nine o'clock the rumour had reached most of the bigger houses and was being discussed and commented upon at the breakfast table. Most people were pleased, for the Dower House had stood empty for nearly a year—ever since old Miss Morven died —and it would be pleasant to see the house occupied again, especially if the newcomers were " nice " ; but some of the older people were not so pleased. It seemed wrong that Mr. Morven should sell the Dower House, which was part of the estate. He should have leased it—perhaps he *had* leased it—after all, the whole thing was only a rumour and as such to be accepted with a grain of salt.

It was a windy March morning. Mr. Morven came out of his south gate, which opened straight onto the village street, and set off through the village at a brisk pace. As usual he had two dogs at his heels, two brown cockers with curly coats, who followed him like two brown shadows. Quite a number of people, who were shopping or talking or hurrying home with full baskets, saw Mr. Morven and greeted him ; some of them commented on the weather— a peck of March dust is worth a king's ransom—but although every one was burning to ask whether or not the rumour was true and if so who had bought Dower House and when they were coming and a dozen other questions, nobody had the temerity to do so. This was all the more curious because Richard Morven was a friendly person and his neighbours liked him. They were proud of him, too, for he was a " proper squire." He looked a squire, tall and well-made with greying hair and fine eyes, and he behaved as a squire should, which is to say he was always polite and pleasant and well-mannered in a slightly old-fashioned way. Perhaps it was this slightly old-fashioned way of his which protected him from the curiosity of his neighbours.

Miss Crease was different, of course ; for one thing she was old and ugly, and for another she had known Richard Morven since the day he was born. She was in her garden when she saw him walking down the street and she called and beckoned to him in a peremptory manner.

Richard Morven stopped at once, crossed the street and leant upon the gate ; the spaniels sat down one on either side and waited patiently.

" You've sold Dower House, they say," said Miss Crease, hobbling across the grass. " I hope you've got a good thumping price for it. Who have you sold it to and when are they coming ? Are they going to do it up or what ? "

" Bush telegraph," said Richard Morven, smiling. He had a very charming smile which crinkled up the corners of his eyes.

" Bush telegraph or grape-vine or something," agreed Miss Crease. " It's quite odd, isn't it ? They know more about you than you know yourself."

" Quite odd . . . so that was why ! I had a curious feeling as I came through the village, as if . . . as if . . ."

" I know," nodded Miss Crease. " And of course they *were* all talking about you and trying to make up their minds to tackle you about it—but nobody dared, except me." She gave a little cackle of amusement at her own temerity.

" How did they know ! " said Richard thoughtfully. " How *could* they know ? "

" So it's true ? "

" Perfectly true. I sold it yesterday through my lawyers in London. The purchaser is a lady."

" Is she pretty ? " demanded Miss Crease.

Richard Morven was taken aback. The question seemed an extraordinary one coming from Miss Crease. He had expected questions, of course, for Miss Crease was of an inquisitive nature, but not this question. She was so incredibly ugly herself, and always had been . . . but perhaps that was why, thought Richard vaguely.

" Is she pretty ? " repeated Miss Crease.

" Does it matter ? " asked Richard.

" Of course it matters. Dr. Johnson said beauty in itself is estimable and should be respected—or words to that effect. I ask you for the third time, is she pretty ? "

Richard smiled. " I don't know," he said. " Lawyers don't tell you things like that. They're more interested in the colour of the lady's money than the colour of her hair."

" Pshaw ! " exclaimed Miss Crease in disgust.

" Quite," said Richard gravely. " I agree with you. It would be interesting to know whether or not my new neighbour is pleasant to look at."

" Interesting ! " cried Miss Crease with an upward inflexion. " It's essential. Don't you know *anything* about her, Richard ? "

" Nothing except that she lives in London, is obviously well off and very impulsive."

" Impulsive ? " cried Miss Crease, seizing upon the word.

" She bought the house as if it were—a bun. She bought it straight off without seeing it."

" She must be mad ! " cried Miss Crease incredulously.

" Houses are scarce," he reminded her.

There was a short silence.

" Richard," said Miss Crease at last in quite a different tone. " Richard, were you wise ? She may be a horrible person. She may be young and entertain hordes of " bright young things " who will rush madly about the village in noisy cars. She may be old and disagreeable. The Dower House is next door to me ; it is actually in your grounds. Oh, I know it has a high wall all round and a separate entrance, but still . . ." She paused and looked at him.

" Yes," he agreed. " Yes, I know. I didn't mean to sell it like that to somebody I knew nothing about. I thought people would come down and see it—and all that. But once I had told Dickson and Weller to sell the place it was out of my hands. They sold it. I suppose I couldn't really complain."

" Did you complain ? "

" I hadn't the face," admitted Richard with a deprecating smile.

" Oh, well, perhaps it will get you out of your rut."

" But I like my rut ! I was thankful to get back into my nice comfortable rut as soon as the war was over. My rut fits me perfectly. Nothing shall dig me out."

" I like mine, too, but there's an excuse for me. I'm old," said Miss Crease.

" I'm getting old," smiled Richard.

" You're forty-five," said Miss Crease firmly. " You're a mere child. It seems only yesterday you came to see me with your mother and ate sugar biscuits. Do you ever hear from your wife ? "

" Occasionally," said Richard Morven, closing up like an oyster.

Miss Crease was old and ugly and therefore licensed to be inquisitive and to rush in where angels feared to tread, but she knew that this time she had gone too far. But anyhow I got *something* out of him, thought Miss Crease as she watched him walk away.

Continuing his walk, Richard thought over the con-

versation. He had been uneasy before and his old friend's
trenchant remarks had increased his discomfort. Perhaps
he had been foolish . . . but he had never dreamt that the
house would be sold straight off like that in a matter of
hours without any of the usual preliminaries. It would be
most annoying if the new owner disturbed the even tenor
of life at Old Quinings. Richard Morven was wedded to
peace and quiet, he had his books, his garden and his dogs
—he wanted no more. Mr. and Mrs. Haygarth, an in-
valuable couple, looked after him and made him extremely
comfortable. Richard had spent the war in an adminis-
trative post, he had been swept into it willy-nilly at the
beginning, but although he had to live in Bath to be near
his work he was able to get home for week-ends. The
Haygarths were over-age for war service so they had kept
the Manor open. It had worked out well.

Richard strode on. He had taken the path which led
across the moor, and the breeze and the sunshine began to
raise his spirits. The thing was done—and why imagine
unpleasant consequences? It was natural to suppose that
only a woman who liked a quiet country life would buy a
house in a quiet country village. Very well then, why
worry? Miss Crease was old and crotchety . . . she was
getting positively childish, thought Richard. It was unpardonable of her to mention Wanda . . . like that . . . quite
suddenly . . . quite irrelevantly. Richard preferred not to
think about his wife. He had discovered that if one really
made up one's mind firmly enough one could stop thinking
about a subject which gave one pain. He had done so
years ago—it was galling to find that other people still
thought about Wanda, discussed her.

Richard decapitated a thistle with his stick. He was
upset and Miss Crease's inconsiderate remark had brought
Wanda clearly to his mind. He could not dismiss her
image. . . . Very well, he would think of her deliberately.

Although it was now more than fourteen years ago
Richard remembered every detail of the evening he had
first seen Wanda. It was at the Savoy. He was asked to

join a party for supper after the theatre and Wanda was one of the party. She was absolutely beautiful, breath-takingly beautiful ; Richard had never seen anything or anybody so beautiful before—no wonder he had fallen in love with her. Wanda had been swept off her feet by Richard's adoration and in a few months they were married. At first they were happy together but not for long ; Richard soon began to realise that the quiet life at Old Quinings was boring Wanda ; she was half American and used to her own way ; she was used to gaiety and admiration. The fact was, thought Richard as he strode along, he and Wanda were not really companions. Wanda was so lovely to look at that he had credited her with a depth of soul she did not possess . . . he did not know what Wanda had thought about him but he was aware that he had not come up to her expectations as a husband. She found Old Quinings dull—that was the real trouble. When once she had redecorated the Manor and installed the ultra-modern plumbing she considered essential, there was nothing left for her to do, no outlet for her abounding vitality. Wanda liked travelling, Richard preferred to stay at home, so they drifted into the habit of doing as they pleased without reference to each other. This was all the easier because Wanda had money of her own and therefore was com-pletely independent. There was no definite break (as far as Richard could remember, the matter had not even been discussed between them), there was no unpleasantness at all. They just drifted into the arrangement. Wanda had hosts of friends who continually asked her to go with them to Cannes, or Egypt or Scotland ; at first Richard was asked too, but as he always refused and Wanda accepted rap-turously it became natural to leave him out of the invitation. Old Quinings remained Wanda's home ; she returned when she wanted a peaceful interlude and lived with Richard quite happily. In fact she made it clear that she liked her home and her husband quite a lot as long as she was free to leave them when the spirit moved her.

Their daughter was born in 1937 ; they called her

Susan after Richard's mother. Wanda had not intended to have a child but she behaved quite well about it, and she was so strong and healthy that she was soon as fit as ever and if possible more beautiful than before. She engaged a competent nurse for Susan and went off to Egypt for the winter. Munich put a stop to Wanda's activities; she decided that Europe was too unsettled to be comfortable and turned her eyes west. She had countless relatives in America, all clamouring for her to come and bring Susan with her—Susan's maternal grandmother had never seen the child. Richard saw no reason why they should not go; he did not intend to leave his home, of course, but he and Wanda were used to separation. Wanda considered the matter for a few days and then packed up and departed, taking Susan and the nurse as part of her mountainous baggage. Richard had seen them off at Tilbury and he had not seen them since.

He had heard from Wanda quite frequently at first; when the war started she wrote urging him to come. Britain was finished, wrote Wanda, every one in the States was certain of that. Richard disagreed with these views, and in any case he felt that if Britain was done for he would rather go down with Britain than watch her downfall from a foreign shore. He wrote and told Wanda what he felt and stayed at home. Several other letters passed between them, letters tinged with bitterness, for they could not understand one another's point of view. This was the first real disagreement between them, it was the first time they had found a subject important enough to rouse their passions.

The bitterness passed, of course (it passed when the United States entered the war), but the fact that they had disagreed so profoundly left an unpleasant feeling behind. Lately Richard had heard from Wanda again; her letters were colourless, they did not express her personality; she told him very little of interest about herself and her affairs.

Richard went over all this as he walked along and was so absorbed in his thoughts that he failed to observe the activities of his spaniels. They had got bored with following and gone off to find something more interesting. A rabbit had run across the path . . . what more natural than to follow the scent and search for it amongst the brambles? What indeed? They were seeking diligently— it was unfortunate that Cora should have found it necessary to give tongue.

Richard stopped and looked back. Where were those confounded dogs? He put two fingers to his mouth and whistled loudly. The next moment the brambles were swept aside and the two brown shadows appeared, looking somewhat guilty and ashamed. They had deserted their god to attend to their own affairs.

"Bad dogs!" said Richard. "A rabbit, I suppose?"

Cora wagged her tail.

CHAPTER TWO

"The new lady 'as come to the Dower House," said Haygarth in a conversational tone as he handed Mr. Morven the potatoes.

"What!" exclaimed Richard Morven in amazement. "Do you mean she's *there*? When did the furniture come?"

Haygarth's lean, lugubrious countenance brightened into something very like a smile. It was agreeable to surprise Mr. Morven, to have news to retail which really interested him. "No furniture 'as come, sir," said Haygarth, making the most of his opportunity.

"But that's impossible! She can't be living in the house without any furniture. She must be staying at the Bull and Bush."

"She is staying at the Dower House," declared Haygarth.

"How do you know?"

"The village told me," said Haygarth solemnly. "The village 'as seen the lady going in and out. No furniture

vans 'as come. The village is definite on that point, sir—
quite definite."

Richard helped himself to the potatoes and thought
about the matter. It was most extraordinary that Miss
Hardy should come to Old Quinings and take up her
abode in a completely empty house—it was almost incred-
ible. If Mrs. Haygarth had been his informant he would
have taken the story with a grain of salt, for Mrs. Haygarth
was fat and chatty and loved a bit of gossip (she loved
gossip for its own sake and did not mind whether or not it
was true), but Haygarth was reliable and not given to
exaggeration.

"I had better go over after dinner," said Richard
Morven suddenly. "She might want something. I'll take
the key of the side door. Don't wait up, Haygarth."

"Very good, sir," said Haygarth.

It was a fine night ; moonlit, with a touch of frost in
the air. Richard lighted a cigar and walked down the path
to the Dower House. It was a well-known path ; his feet
knew every inch of the way, for old Miss Morven had
expected her nephew to visit her daily and had been very
much annoyed if he failed in his duty towards her. Richard
had an odd feeling that he was going to see Aunt Ellen ;
he knew he was not, of course, for he had been with the
old lady when she died ; he had seen her buried in the
family vault and superintended the dismantling of the
house.

Aunt Ellen had gone, the furniture had gone and the
house was no longer his. He disliked the idea intensely. It
seemed wrong. It seemed even worse when he went through
the green door in the wall and saw the house before him in
the moonlight . . . it was such a lovely little house, so
gracious and dignified. It was older than the Manor (not
less than three hundred years old) ; it had been built by
Morvens for Morvens to live in and now a Morven had
sold it. He felt a traitor.

The bell was hidden in the ivy—Richard was not
acquainted with the bell—but he found it at last and rang

it, and a few moments later the door opened and the new owner appeared.

" I'm Richard Morven," said Richard, who had rehearsed his speech with care. " I heard you had come and I wondered if I could do anything to help you. You are Miss Hardy, I suppose."

" Yes," said Miss Hardy. " Yes, I'm Kate Hardy. It's very kind of you—will you come in ? "

He could not see her very well, but he liked her voice. It was low and clear and cordial. He had a feeling that she was really pleased to see him ; so he went in. The hall was completely empty and very dirty. Wisps of straw were lying about and there was a fusty smell in the air.

" You aren't living here ! " exclaimed Richard involuntarily.

Miss Hardy laughed. She had an attractive laugh, infectious and chuckling. " Isn't it awful," she agreed. " But I've cleaned up the morning-room and I can offer you a chair."

He followed her into the little morning-room without speaking ; he was too surprised to speak. The morning-room was clean ; there was a fire burning in the grate. There was a camp-bed in the corner. A canvas chair stood beside the fire and near it a packing-case with a cup and saucer and a plate laid out upon it.

" Do sit down, Mr. Morven," said Miss Hardy, indicating the chair.

" But won't you——"

" I prefer the floor," she declared, subsiding on to the floor in front of the fire. " Yes, really—I'm quite comfortable here."

Richard looked at her and saw it was true. She was comfortable. She sat there with one leg bent beneath her and one arm supporting her. He took the chair. He was feeling slightly dazed. The morning-room was where Aunt Ellen always sat, surrounded by her treasures. It had been full of furniture in Aunt Ellen's day, so full that one could hardly move . . . full of tables with knick-knacks upon them, full of old-fashioned chairs and hassocks ; the cabinet was full of china and the parrot's cage had stood on the top of it ; the mantelpiece was draped with an embroidered cloth (which had a fringe of little woollen balls) and was crowded with photographs and ornaments. Richard seemed to see that full room superimposed upon this empty one. It was a curious experience, and the most curious part was that Richard preferred the empty room. You could see its shape better, he decided.

" It's a beautifully proportioned room," said Miss Hardy, sensing Richard's thought.

Richard said he was glad she liked it.

" Of course I like it," she declared. " Who wouldn't ? It's a lovely house."

There was a short silence. Neither of them was embarrassed by the silence, for it was a perfectly comfortable one. Miss Hardy was looking at the fire which burned brightly and cosily in the old-fashioned grate ; Richard was looking at Miss Hardy and wondering about her. He decided that he liked her immensely ; he liked her unselfconsciousness. Most people would have thought it necessary to apologise for bringing him into an empty house and offering him a canvas chair to sit on. Miss Hardy had made no attempt to apologise ; she saw no reason to apologise, and there was none : Richard had come of his own accord and she had welcomed him and given him her chair; it was as simple as that. She was simple, then . . . but she was also extremely intelligent, for she had divined his thought in a moment and answered it. He looked at her with interest. She was neither old and disagreeable—as Miss Crease had feared—nor was she a " bright young thing." He guessed her age as thirty. She was tall and very thin, almost ungainly ; her bones showed more than is usual beneath their covering of skin, but they were good bones. She was certainly not pretty, thought Richard with an involuntary smile. At first glance he had received the impression that she was definitely ugly, but now he was revising the impression . . . there was beauty in the modelling of her face (in the curve of her jaw and the poise of her neck and the setting of her ear), beauty of line. Her mouth was too wide, but you forgot that when she smiled.

Suddenly she began to talk. "It was nice of you to come," she said. "It can't be pleasant for you to come to the house now that it doesn't belong to you."

"I shall have to get used to that," replied Richard. "As I told you, I wondered if there was anything we could do——"

"Don't worry," she said quickly. "I chose to come with my eyes wide open ; I knew it wouldn't be comfortable."

"You don't care about comfort ? "

"Oh, yes, I do," declared Miss Hardy, turning her head and looking up at him. "I like comfort, and I intend to be very comfortable here when I get my furniture out of store and everything arranged, but there are other things that matter more, aren't there ? I wanted to get out of town—I felt I had to."

"Was that why you bought the house so—quickly ? "

"So recklessly," amended Miss Hardy, laughing. "Yes, of course. Mr. Chester, my lawyer, thought I was mad . . . and having bought the house I simply couldn't rest until I had seen it. So I packed and came."

"Why did you suddenly want to leave London ? " It was an impertinent question ; Richard was aghast when he heard himself uttering it, but Miss Hardy did not seem to mind.

"It wasn't so very sudden," she said in a thoughtful tone. "I've thought about it off and on for a long time, but I've lived in London all my life and I couldn't leave it during the war, because . . . because . . ."

"Because you couldn't leave an old friend in trouble."

"Something like that, I suppose," admitted Miss Hardy. She gathered up her knees and put her arms round them ; it was an unconscious movement, swift and graceful. The woman seemed to have no bones, thought Richard, who disliked sitting upon the floor.

" I thought about it off and on for a long time," she continued. " Life in town is so artificial, you can pick and choose your friends ; you needn't have anything to do with the woman who lives next door if you don't like the look of her."

Richard laughed and said, " You may not like the look of Miss Crease—she's your nearest neighbour—but you'll have a good deal to do with her, I expect."

" Exactly ! That's my point. You may not have much in common with your neighbours but you can't ignore them. The mere fact of trying to find something in common is good. It enlarges you. A small country place is a world in miniature, there are *all* kinds of people in it and you get to know them all . . . you can't just keep to your own kind of people. Is that true ? "

" Yes," said Richard.

" Besides," said Miss Hardy thoughtfully. " Besides, I've begun to wonder what my own kind *is*. I've begun to find life a little boring. It will be quite different here, there will be people for me to help and people who will help me ; there will be interesting people, dull people, crazy people —all individuals, all real and worth while. In town you spend your leisure rushing about doing things ; in the country you stay put and *live*."

" How do you know ? " asked Richard.

" Yes, that's funny," agreed Miss Hardy. " I must have imagined it, I suppose. Have I imagined it rightly, Mr. Morven ? "

He thought she had. It was his own idea of Old Quinings : a world in miniature with good and evil, sense and nonsense mixed up together in confusion. He hoped she would like the mixture, he thought she would find it interesting if nothing else.

" Real people are always interesting," continued Miss Hardy. " The trouble with so many people nowadays is that they aren't real, they don't think for themselves. They accept a label from somebody else and wear it. In the old days each person was himself, an individual with an immortal soul. When you think about it seriously that is a belief which gives a man the right to feel important. It gives him a sense of his own value ; and a man who values himself will never accept a label from somebody else and wear it."

" He makes his own label."

" He doesn't need a label at all ! " cried Miss Hardy. " He's himself—take him or leave him—he's a man with an immortal soul."

She elaborated her theme. There she sat and talked with no thought for herself—nor for her guest either, as he very well knew—she was completely absorbed in what she was saying. Her long thin hands were clasped round her knees ; now and then she threw back her head in an unconscious gesture. Her hair in the fire-glow looked red ; but it was not red, it was true brown. Thick and shining and perfectly straight ; except for one deep wave, it swept back and was knotted loosely at the nape of her neck.

"Now tell me about the house," said Miss Hardy suddenly. " It's a darling house ; I love it. I want to know all about it."

Richard told her what he could and promised to let her see the records which would tell her more. " It has always been a Dower House," he said. " Henry Morven built it for his mother about three hundred years ago and since then it has been used by the family either for a dispossessed parent or for some other relative who needed accommodation. My old aunt was the last person to live here. She was rather a terrifying old lady and lived to a great age."

" She had a cat, I hope ? "

" Yes," said Richard, smiling. " She had a cat and a parrot. The cat had to be renewed, now and then, but the parrot outlived her. I sent it to the Bull and Bush. Mrs. Gray says it is learning to say some very queer things."

" That's the inn at the end of the village, isn't it ? "

Richard nodded.

" Ghosts ? " inquired Miss Hardy.

" Oh, well——" said Richard, looking at her doubtfully. " You know what it is. I don't think Selina Morven will bother you. Are you going to be in the house alone ? "

" Just for a few days. I like being alone . . . as a matter of fact nobody knows where I am; they'll be furious when they find I've gone."

" They ? " asked Richard. Somehow he could not imagine her as part of a family; she seemed complete in herself.

" My sister and my niece," explained Miss Hardy. " They've been staying with me in my flat since the war ended. They like town. Martha Body will come here, of course—at least I'm almost sure she will. She's a splendid person. She looks after me and keeps me from doing mad things. She would have insisted upon seeing the Dower House before buying it, so I haven't told her a word about it. Poor Martha, but it was the best way and saved a lot of bother. And after all," said Miss Hardy defiantly. " After all, it's my own money—and what *is* the use of making a lot of money if you can't spend it as you want ? "

Richard nodded. He was slightly muddled by this sudden spate of information and was trying to sort it out and form it into a reasonable background for the personality of his new friend, but he found it difficult, for she continued to talk and her conversation was so compelling that it swept him along and demanded his whole attention.

" I wish I could ask you to stay at the Manor," said Richard suddenly. " It would be so much more comfortable—and sensible, really—but my wife isn't at home."

" I shall look forward to meeting her," said Miss Hardy politely.

" She doesn't live with me," Richard said.

There was a short pause and then Richard decided to tell Miss Hardy the whole story. If he did not tell her someone else would, and he had no idea what Old Quinings thought about himself and Wanda. It was difficult to begin, but after he had overcome that first difficulty he found himself telling Miss Hardy everything quite naturally and without reservations. She was interested, he could see, and her questions were very much to the point. She was not elaborately tactful, he would have hated that, nor did she commiserate with him at Wanda's expense, but she gave him sympathetic understanding and a new point of view. She understood that what galled Richard was the fact that he had not been able to make his marriage a success, and without absolving him from blame—for there are always two sides to a question—she showed him that marriage between two people with such divergent views was bound to be a failure.

"I always hoped she would settle down in time," said Richard, rather wretchedly. "It was that misunderstanding about the results of the war that finished everything. I saw then that it was hopeless. She didn't even try to understand my point of view."

"How could she understand!" cried Miss Hardy. "She was a cosmopolitan, she had no tradition of any kind —you come of a long line of English Squires, you're rooted in English soil. To my mind that misunderstanding—or something like it—was bound to take place sooner or later; it would have taken place before if anything had arisen which seemed important to you both. Your marriage was a failure from the beginning. It could never have been anything else."

"Yes," said Richard, thoughtfully—for Miss Hardy had given him something to think about—"yes, you're right, of course. Success was impossible from the beginning, our values were different. We couldn't understand one another's point of view. It was a wretched affair."

"The person I'm sorry for is Susan," said Miss Hardy, gazing at the fire.

Richard was so astounded that he was dumb.

"Susan didn't ask to be born," continued Miss Hardy reasonably. "She may be quite happy, of course, but on the other hand she may be miserable."

"She's just a baby!" Richard exclaimed . . . and then

he paused. Susan must be nine years old! He had a daughter of nine years old and he had no idea what she was like! It was odd that he had not thought of Susan before, but Susan was part of the " mess " which he had dismissed from his mind—that was the reason. And as a matter of fact, Richard had never been interested in Susan, nor had he thought of her as a person. He had been disappointed that she was not a boy to inherit the Morven estates and carry on the line, all the more disappointed because he knew Wanda would take good care not to have another child. Richard liked kittens and puppies, he found them most attractive, but there was nothing attractive about his daughter. She was small and plain and completely bald and her complexion was atrocious. He did not see much of her, of course, for the competent nurse discouraged visits to the nursery, but it seemed to Richard that every time he looked at the baby it cried or was sick . . . yet he was assured it was a healthy child and was making good progress.

" She's a Morven, isn't she ? " said Miss Hardy, breaking the little silence.

" Yes," said Richard dazedly. " Yes, of course."

" Well then," said Miss Hardy.

Richard was silent. He saw the implications : he had fathered a child, handing on inherited traits which might make a nomadic existence unbearable . . . handing on the traditions of a long line of English Squires. The Morven blood ran in Susan's veins just as certainly as if she had been a son. " But I don't see what I can do," added Richard with a sigh.

Miss Hardy made coffee (perhaps she thought her guest needed refreshment after his shock) and they drank it and smoked and talked about various matters of interest to them both. It seemed perfectly natural to sit here, talking, but when Richard rose to go he was recalled to a sense of time and place and remembered the conventions.

" Good heavens ! " he exclaimed. " It's after one ! "

After one o'clock did not seem late to the town mouse,

but she took the point and laughed. "Old Quinings wouldn't approve?"

"Old Quinings must never know," declared Richard, smiling uncertainly. "It's unpardonable of me ... honestly, Miss Hardy, nobody must ever know that we have been chatting for hours like this——"

"In my bedroom," added Miss Hardy, glancing at the camp-bed.

Richard tried to laugh.

"Of course," continued Miss Hardy, nodding. "I quite understand. Nobody shall ever know. I suppose Miss Crease would be horrified?"

"Horrified is not the word," said Richard, trying to speak lightly.

"Dear Miss Crease," said Miss Hardy. "I feel as if I know her already; I'm sure I shall like her enormously. This is going to be fun."

They crossed the hall together. Richard opened the front door and stepped out.

"A lovely night," remarked Miss Hardy, sniffing the air appreciatively.

"Lovely," agreed Richard. "Good-night and thank you—thank you for everything."

"Good-night," responded Miss Hardy. "Oh, by the way, I suppose I had better tell you before you go. It seems unfair not to—and you're sure to find it out sooner or later."

"What?" asked Richard, pausing on the step.

"Don't look so alarmed, it's nothing very desperate," said Miss Hardy, laughing. "I'm not a vampire—nor even a crook. I write, that's all."

"Write!" echoed Richard.

"Books," said Miss Hardy, shutting the door.

Richard stood for a moment looking at the closed door, then he put on his hat and turned away. He might have guessed (thought Richard as he walked home). He certainly might have known she did *something*, for she had about her an air of achievement. She wore an air of assurance which can only come from personal success. Richard was sure her books were successful, not only because of her remark about " making a lot of money " which had puzzled him at the time, but also because he had felt her power. She had immense vitality, a boundless interest in life and an amazing understanding of her fellow-creatures. Kate Hardy—he knew no author of that name, but perhaps she wrote under another name. He must ask her. He wanted to read her books. He wanted to ask a thousand questions. Had she realised this and deliberately kept her piece of information until he was out of the house so that she could shut the door between them, or was it really an after-thought? He tried to decide which it was, but he couldn't. He didn't know enough about her.

CHAPTER THREE

KATE HARDY slept well, untroubled by the ghost of Selina Morven. She slept for six hours, which was enough, and woke feeling refreshed and ready for a new day. The day was there, waiting for her. She could see the garden through the open window; it was bathed in golden sunshine. Kate always woke early, it was a natural habit. She could remember waking early as a child and watching the room lighten as the sun rose. In those days she had entertained herself with stories, which went on from day to day and passed the time very pleasantly, so pleasantly that she was almost sorry when her nurse came to get her dressed. The habit of waking early was still with her, and these early morning hours were immensely valuable to her. She lay in bed and thought about her books. All her real work was done then; problems of plot and character were solved and the day's work planned so that when she sat down at her desk there was nothing to do except write. Kate some-times wondered whether she woke early because she wrote, or wrote because she woke early.

This morning, however, Kate did not lie in bed and work. She was on holiday. She rose and dressed, made herself some tea and boiled an egg (she had managed to buy some in Old Quinings). To-day was Sunday, of course. Perhaps that accounted for the quietness. It was very quiet. The only sound was the lowing of a cow in the distance. A dog barked once and was silent. Kate was so anxious to go out and explore that she could hardly spare the time to eat. She left the dishes to wash later and ran out into the garden. How fresh it was ! How magical ! And it was hers. She had never owned a tree before—it seemed wonderful to own trees. She ran across the grass and embraced the huge bole of the beech tree, laughing at herself for her foolishness. The grass was wet with rime but the sun was already warm ; the sky was blue and cloudless above the bare branches of Kate's trees. Smoke rose lazily from Kate's chimney and hung like grey gauze in the still air. Kate was so happy that she could hardly bear it, her heart was big with happiness, she felt good, she felt at one with the world. This was worth waiting for. If she died now it would have been worth living. If she had been miserable all her life— and of course she had not—this moment would have made up for it.

The garden of the Dower House was about an acre and was encircled by a high brick wall except upon the north side where it was bounded by a little stream. Beyond the stream was a paddock, which sloped up to a wooden barn with a thatched roof. The paddock and the barn were part of Kate's domain ; Mr. Morven had said so. Kate crossed the stream by some stepping-stones and approached the barn. She opened the door and looked in. It was a delightful place, dim and shadowy, with a scent of hay. A sunbeam glinted through a chink in the old beams. It was like a sword . . . no, thought Kate, rejecting the metaphor, it was not *like* anything, it was perfect in itself : a ray of sunshine with little specks of dust dancing in it. In one corner of the barn there was a pronged fork, leaning against the wall, and the ray of light had caught one of the prongs

so that it shone like silver. The floor was softer than the
finest carpet and more beautiful, Kate thought. It was
covered with tiny seeds of grass . . . millions of them. She
took a handful and let them trickle between her fingers . . .
millions of tiny seeds, each one an embryo plant of grass
(so she supposed), each one alive and capable of bearing
fruit, more seeds which in turn could bear others, so that
in the course of time it could cover the whole earth.

There was dust in the rafters, and cobwebs, but that was
as it should be. Dust and cobwebs were right in a barn.
In a house one had to battle against dust and cobwebs ; they
were enemies. Here they were friends.

Kate was suddenly aware of an IDEA lurking in the
recesses of her mind. It was an idea for a story, a magnificent
idea. She saw it for a moment, vague but shining, and then
she turned her mind away from it and shut it out. She had
no time for ideas now, but that was not the only reason,
not even the chief reason. Kate turned her mind from the
idea for fear of frightening it away. Ideas were timid
creatures—like fawns. It would come again, of course, when
she was least expecting it and it would be bolder next time.
She would get a glimpse of it as it came out of the thicket,
before it saw her and bounded away . . . and then, next
time, she would throw it a few crumbs (did fawns eat
crumbs) and get a good look at it while it nosed them and
licked them up with its little tongue. That was how it was
done. Kate sighed. Would she be able to tame it ? She
knew, only too well, that ideas looked more attractive when
they were vague . . . fawns were more attractive when they
were wild. When you caught them they weren't nearly so
pretty. Why was that ? Why should catching them rub off
their bloom ?

Kate laughed aloud at the mixture of metaphors and
tossed a handful of seeds into the air.

" Ah ! " said a voice behind her. " That's funny,
that is."

Kate turned quickly and saw a little old man standing
in the doorway.

He said again, " That's funny, that is," and cackled with laughter. He was thin and bent and his face was like a wizened apple, creased and furrowed. He was earthy, as if he had spent his whole life amongst earth, working in it, sleeping in it. His eyes were bright and beady and restless like the eyes of a small wild animal.

" What was funny ? " asked Kate.

He stooped and made the motion of tossing handfuls of chaff, looking at her sidelong as he did so. He seemed to think she would understand, but Kate had no idea what he meant. Abandoning the subject (which seemed at a dead end, for the man either would not or could not explain) Kate asked him his name and learned that it was Abijah Rannish and that he lived with his granddaughter in a small cottage on the Morven estate. There was no need to explain who she was ; Abijah knew. She had a feeling that he knew everything about her—but of course that was absurd.

By this time the sun was high and warm. Kate left Abijah in the barn and found a path which strayed happily across a very green meadow full of cows. She found a little river, sliding between shallow green banks. She crossed a hump-backed bridge and sat down on a wooden bench beneath a chestnut tree and looked about her. Across the meadow lay Old Quinings village sleeping amongst elms, and, beyond that, fields, brown and rich with a faint haze of green upon them ; they rose to a shallow ridge crowned with trees. This is England, thought Kate. It was the England Gray had written about and Constable had painted. Piccadilly Circus seemed a million miles away.

She sat there for quite a long time steeping herself in peace and then rose and approached the village . . . there were more trees on the green and in the wide street. An old man sat before his cottage door with his legs apart and his hands clasped upon the handle of his stick. He greeted her as she passed. The Bull and Bush was at the end of the street, an old house but well kept and newly painted. Kate pushed open the door, which was silver with age, and

found herself looking into a pleasant room, full of sunshine.
You had to step down into the room over a lintel-step
hollowed by wear. In the window was a pink geranium.
A parrot sat on a stand ; its bright beady eyes twinkled at
Kate. " 'Ave another 'alf pint," it suggested hoarsely.

Kate laughed and at that moment a girl came out of a
swing door. She was a tall girl with dark hair and fine
eyes, her bare arms were strong and shapely.

" Can I have lunch ? " asked Kate, adding on a sudden
impulse, " I suppose you couldn't let me have a room here
for a few days."

" You can have lunch," said the girl, smiling pleasantly.
" We haven't a room, I'm afraid. I'll ask Mrs. Gray but
I'm afraid it's hopeless."

Kate was given a table in the window and made a very
good meal of cold beef and pickles and apple tart. She
drank a glass of ale and chatted to the girl, and felt at peace
with the world. The girl's name was Mary Stack.

" I suppose you know who I am," said Kate as she
lighted a cigarette.

" The new lady at the Dower House," said the girl
promptly. " Every one knows every one in Old Quinings.
They'll all ask me what you're like."

" I hope you'll give me a good character," Kate said
gravely.

The girl laughed. She had a merry laugh and her wide,
freckled face was full of humour. " They won't get much
out of me," she declared. " Mrs. Gray doesn't like gossip—
it doesn't do in a place like this. I don't live in, you see.
I live with mother—she's gatekeeper at the South Lodge,
quite near you, that is. If you wanted a help with cleaning
I could do a bit after hours."

Kate accepted the offer rapturously. She was very
anxious to get the house cleaned up before she brought
Martha to see it. Mary Stack looked strong and capable ;
she would be a valuable assistant.

While they were talking the parrot had been silent,
eating a small piece of fruit which Mary had put in its dish,

but now as Kate rose to go it declared in a shrill voice, " That's our ghost ! " and followed this somewhat startling announcement with a cackling laugh.

" Isn't he awful ! " said Mary apologetically. " It gives you quite a turn sometimes. He used to belong to old Miss Morven at the Dower House and he copies her to the life. She was rather a terror, Miss Morven was ; very kind in her own way but liked you to do exactly what she said. I was housemaid there before I came to Mrs. Gray."

" Did you ever see the ghost ? " asked its new hostess with interest.

" Not me," replied Mary, laughing. " But Miss Morven used to see it sometimes. She was rather proud of it, I think. There was a picture in the dining-room—a very nice picture of a pretty girl with fair hair and a pink dress—and Miss Morven used to point to it when people came to lunch and say, ' That's our ghost.' "

" That's our ghost ! " repeated the parrot instantly.

" You see ! " said Mary, smiling.

When Kate opened the door in the high wall and went into her own garden she felt she was going home. There was a welcome here. The garden was neglected but she would get it right in time. The house was lovely, its gracious proportions charmed the eye . . . the doors and window-panes needed paint and she must get someone to look at the roof, but there was no hurry. She had all the time in the world to spend upon her new acquisition and plenty of money. She stood for a few minutes looking at her house and enjoying the feeling of ownership . . . and then she heard the " click " of the side gate and saw a woman coming towards her across the lawn.

She was a large comfortable-looking woman in a snowy-white apron; everything about her was extremely clean and neat. Her hair was silver, it was braided and pinned tightly round her head, her face was round and rosy. As she approached, coming from beneath the shadows of the trees into the sunshine, the sun shone down upon her silver hair and snowy apron with positively dazzling effect.

Kate stood and waited for her ; it was obvious that she had something to say.

" I could let you have a room," said the woman shyly. " It might not suit, of course. It's my son's room. He isn't home yet. He's in India."

" But how kind ! " exclaimed Kate.

" It was Mary," she explained. " Mary said you were asking for a room at the Bull and Bush."

" You must be Mrs. Stack," declared Kate ; and indeed, now that she looked at Mrs. Stack, she could see the resemblance to Mary.

" It would be clean," said Mrs. Stack, looking down at her hands, turning them this way and that and examining them in frowning concentration. " I could promise you that, Miss Hardy. It's a small room and not what you've been accustomed to, but it would be clean."

" Yes," said Kate. " Yes, I'm sure it would be ; and I'm sure it would suit me beautifully. It's very kind of you, Mrs. Stack."

The thing was arranged. Mrs. Stack saw no reason why Miss Hardy should not move in at once ; she went into the house and helped Miss Hardy to repack her suitcase. She was very shy and this made her difficult to talk to. Kate did most of the talking ; she told Mrs. Stack that she had never lived in the country before, always in London.

" Smuts," said Mrs. Stack.

" Oh, yes," agreed Kate. " Smuts are awful. I have a maid called Martha Body and she spends all her time waging war on smuts. I like to have the windows open, and she likes them shut."

" She'll find it quiet here," said Mrs. Stack, taking up the suitcase, which was now ready, and carrying it away.

The Stacks' cottage was all that Kate had expected, which is to say it was comfortably furnished and as clean as a new pin. As she unpacked and laid out her few belong-

ings in the drawers she congratulated herself upon her luck.
This was much better than camping in an empty house and
much better than the Bull and Bush—in fact it was perfect.
Everything was slightly old-fashioned, but none the worse
for that. There was a jug of boiling hot water in the basin
on the washstand, with a clean towel over the top of it.
This was an amenity which Kate had not met for years ;
she was almost afraid to use it, but as it had been put there
for her use it seemed ungrateful not to. She poured the
water into the basin and washed her face and hands. The
gong rang and Kate ran down the steep stair, ready for
supper. Mrs. Stack had offered to lay her meals in the
parlour, but Kate had asked to be allowed to come into the
kitchen, for she was a sociable person and was anxious to
make friends with the Stacks.

There was bacon and eggs and tea for supper and
several kinds of scones and cakes and raspberry jam in a
glass dish. Mrs. Stack was putting the finishing touches to
the table as she went in. Mary had not come home yet.

" It's not what you've been accustomed to," said Mrs.
Stack, bustling about with a flustered air.

" No, it isn't," said Kate, laughing. " It's three times
better than the food we get in London and twice as much.
Do sit down, Mrs. Stack."

Mrs. Stack smiled and sat down. She did the honours
well, pressing her guest to eat the good things she had
provided.

" Try one of these potato scones, Miss," urged Mrs.
Stack. " They're very light—though I say it myself—
Walter always used to say I made them so that they melted
in your mouth. Or have a little cake—they're very small.
You need feeding up, you know. Very thin, you are, very
thin indeed. This is farm butter—it's not what you've
been accustomed to, of course."

" I'm accustomed to a scrape of marge," agreed Kate.

Mrs. Stack laughed quite heartily ; she had begun to
come out of her shell.

Kate was reminded of her nursery days (there was a

pleasant nursery air about the cosy little kitchen) and she
said so.

" Well, that's funny," said Mrs. Stack. " It's funny you
saying that, because that's what I was before I married
Mr. Stack. I was a nanny ; always in very good families,
I was. First I was with Mrs. Pearce as a nursery-maid and
then I went to her sister-in-law—dear little children they
were—and then I went to a friend of Mrs. Pearce, single-
handed."

Now that she had started to talk Mrs. Stack seemed
wound up. Kate heard about the little Pearces and the
little Hays. She was shown their photographs and admired
them. There was a photograph of an officer upon the
draped mantelpiece. Kate asked who that was.

" Oh, that's Walter," said Mrs. Stack with an assumption
of unconcern.

Kate took up the photograph and looked at it. " Your
son ? " she asked.

" Yes," said Mrs. Stack, struggling between pride and
modesty. " Yes, that's Walter. He's like his father—not
like me at all. You see, Miss, he was in the Territorials
before the war—Walter was always keen on soldiers—so
then when the war started he went to France with them
and they made him a lieutenant. He had an awful time
in France. Well, then he came home and was in Scotland
for a bit and then he went out to Burma. He's a major
now," added Mrs. Stack, pride having routed modesty.
" Acting major, he is—you can see his crowns on his shoulder
if you take it near the light."

Kate saw his crowns. She was even more interested in
his face—a strong face, with a good nose and a firm jaw.
The eyes looked at you straight out of the photograph,
gravely humorous.

" I should like to meet Walter," Kate said.

" He was nicely brought up, I *will* say that," declared
his mother. " I saw to that, of course. My children were
well trained from the start—not like some of the other
children about here ; little hooligans with no idea how to

behave themselves. Eat like pigs some of them do ! The ignorance of *some* people about bringing up children you would hardly believe."

Kate hid a smile. It was obvious that Mrs. Stack attributed a good deal of Walter's success to his table manners.

" He was a good scholar, too," continued Mrs. Stack, who (like many mothers) enjoyed talking about her son, and, once she got started upon the enthralling subject, found it difficult to stop. " Composition was his best subject. Mr. Forster—he was the schoolmaster in those days—said Walter had a wonderful grasp of language—that's what he put in Walter's report. And of course he was always reading, a regular book-worm he was ; but he was a real boy for all that," declared his mother with a reminiscent smile. " A real boy, he was. Always full of fun, always getting into boyish scrapes, and then being sorry afterwards. ' Look before you leap, Walter,' I used to say—but Walter used to leap first and then look afterwards."

She laughed and Kate laughed too.

" What Walter liked best was a day on the moor," continued Mrs. Stack. " He used to go with Reuben Doubleday and fish in the stream. Mr. Morven gave them permission, of course. Mr. Morven was always very kind to Walter. Off they would go for the whole day—the two of them together—with a sandwich in their pockets or perhaps one of my pies. Reuben was a nice boy in those days," added Mrs. Stack with a sigh.

Kate listened to all this with no sign of fatigue. She was interested, not so much in the adventures of the two boys whom she had never seen, but more in Mrs. Stack herself. Mrs. Stack was so good, so wholesome. There she sat by the side of the fire, knitting a sock and talking. The clock on the wall ticked on, the atmosphere was cosy. Kate was reminded again of her nursery days, reminded more forcibly than before, for her own " nanny," whom she had dearly loved, had been so very like Mrs. Stack.

" Yes, it's a pity," continued Mrs. Stack, shaking her

head sadly. "It's a pity about Reuben. Reuben's gone down the hill, I'm afraid. You know, Miss Hardy, it was a bad thing for a young chap like Reuben not to go to the war. He didn't volunteer, you see, and then all Mr. Seager's other men left and Reuben couldn't be spared. Well, that's what they said, anyhow. It was a bad thing, I think. Reuben should have gone and let one of the older men stay. It would have made a man of Reuben."

They were still sitting by the fire talking when Mary came in. "Well, there now!" cried Mary cheerfully. "You *do* look cosy and no mistake. I *said* you and Miss Hardy would get on like a house on fire, didn't I, Mother?"

Mrs. Stack actually blushed. "You go and take off your things, Mary," she said. "Your supper's in the oven —dry as a bone by this time. I suppose you met Jack."

"He saw me home," explained Mary; it was her turn to blush.

"You'll get home quicker—*and* safer—by yourself, my girl," said Mrs. Stack firmly.

CHAPTER FOUR

MISS CREASE was in her garden enjoying the spring sunshine when she saw Richard Morven walking down the street, followed, as usual, by two brown spaniels. She beckoned to him in her usual manner and Richard as usual obeyed, but his smile as he leaned upon the gate and waited for Miss Crease to approach was a trifle apprehensive.

"Not pretty," said Miss Crease decisively. "Not pretty —but decidedly interesting. Looks like somebody and knows how to speak. It's astonishing how few of the younger people nowadays know how to speak; they mumble and jumble their words and don't open their mouths, or else they shout at me. I'm not deaf—not in the least—I can hear people perfectly well if they speak correctly."

"Yes, of course," said Richard.

"Have you seen her?"

"Yes, on Saturday night. I looked in to see if there was anything I could do."

"Quite right," said Miss Crease, nodding. "Very neighbourly of you, Richard."

Richard breathed a sigh of relief.

"It's odd that she didn't mention it," added Miss Crease thoughtfully. "I said something about you but she never said she'd met you."

"Never thought of it, I expect," said Richard quickly. "She's busy getting the house cleaned up and all that."

"H'm," said Miss Crease. "H'm—perhaps. I suppose she's at the Bull and Bush—quite comfortable, I believe. In ordinary times one would have had her to stay, of course, but nowadays one can't. Annie seems to think she's over-worked with nothing to do but look after me, so visitors are out of the question. Annie's temper is atrocious."

"Of course," agreed Richard hastily. He did not think Miss Hardy would have been comfortable at Rose Cottage, not on account of Annie's temper, which he believed to be positively angelic, but because Miss Crease was didactic in the extreme. Miss Hardy was neither meek nor particularly tactful ; it would be better if the two ladies met infrequently, Richard thought.

"I don't know why you say *of course*," said Miss Crease pettishly. "It would be the natural thing for me to ask the woman to stay in my house until she got settled in her own. I dislike the appearance of inhospitality more than I can say."

"It *would* have been the natural thing," said Richard soothingly. "But, as you say, it's different nowadays with your reduced staff and the difficulties of rationing."

Miss Crease was appeased. "Oh, well," she said. "One just hopes to heaven she will be comfortable at the Bull and Bush."

Richard hesitated. There had been a questioning inflec-tion in Miss Crease's pious hope. It was quite possible she was trying him out to see if he knew Miss Hardy's movements . . . wiser to be frank, thought Richard. " She has gone to the Stacks'," he said.

" To the Stacks' ! " cried Miss Crease. " What an extraordinary thing to do ! "

" Why extraordinary ? The Lodge is quite comfortable and Mrs. Stack is an excellent cook, and as neither you nor I are able to offer Miss Hardy accommodation she must find it where she can."

" I've told you why I can't. You agreed that I couldn't," complained Miss Crease, somewhat taken aback by Richard's vehemence.

" And I'll tell you why I can't," said Richard. " I can't offer Miss Hardy hospitality, because this place is full of a lot of old tabby cats who would gossip their heads off." He smiled as he spoke to take the edge off his words for he had no wish to quarrel with the old lady.

" Oh, yes . . . well, of course," exclaimed Miss Crease. " Of course *you* couldn't, Richard. It wouldn't be at *all* the proper thing. But I still think it's extraordinary for her to go to the Stacks'. I should never have thought of going to stay at the Lodge Cottage when I was young. I don't think I should have liked it."

" You wouldn't have liked it," agreed Richard. " In those days the Cottage had no water laid on and no indoor sanitation."

There was a moment when things hung in the balance and it was doubtful whether the old lady would decide to be angry or amused . . . and then the humour of it overcame her and she gave her well-known cackle. " Get along with you, Richard," she said.

Richard was annoyed with himself as he walked on. He had allowed himself to be irritated, and being irritated had said far more than he should. The last thing he wanted was gossip about himself and the woman who had come to live at his gate, for gossip was not only a nuisance but it sullied things which were pleasant and innocent. He admired and liked Miss Hardy, but it was doing her no service to champion her hotly either to Miss Crease or to any one else.

He must watch his tongue. He now realised for the first time and with some surprise that he was in a very difficult position, a very vulnerable position, for he was married and yet he had no wife. He was an ideal target for the tabby cats.

Having decided that he must be careful and must see as little as possible of his new neighbour, it was odd that he should turn his steps deliberately towards the Lodge Cottage, but he had been meaning to visit Mrs. Stack for some time past to speak to her about repairs and this seemed a good opportunity.

Mrs. Stack was just coming out. " Oh, Mr. Morven ! " she exclaimed. " Come in, won't you ? I was going up to the Dower House to give Miss Hardy a hand with the cleaning, but there's no hurry about it."

" I won't keep you," Richard said. " I came to tell you about the roof. Seager says the gable is rotten and the wood must be renewed."

" Oh, that ! " said Mrs. Stack. " Don't you worry about that, sir. Walter will be home soon and he'll see to that. He'll make a new gate, too. If Walter can get a few bits of wood he'll soon do all that. We don't want Seager bothering round."

" So Walter is on his way home ? " asked Mr. Morven, smiling. " That will be a great day, won't it ? He's done splendidly. We're all proud of Walter."

Mrs. Stack had locked the door and it was natural that Mr. Morven should turn with her and accompany her to the Dower House. They talked about Walter as they went (Mr. Morven suiting his stride to Mrs. Stack's toddling steps), and they were still talking about Walter when they reached the Dower House and went in through the open door into the cleanly scrubbed hall. Sounds of movement came from the kitchen premises, and, following Mrs. Stack, Richard found himself in a part of the house with which he was unfamiliar. It seemed odd that he had owned the house and known it all his life and had to wait until he had sold it before seeing the kitchen premises.

The house had quite a different feeling to-day. All the windows were open and the whole place seemed larger than he remembered it, larger and brighter and more airy. The kitchen was an exceedingly pleasant room, facing north.

" Is that you, Mrs. Stack ! " cried Kate Hardy, emerging from the scullery attired in a coloured overall with a red handkerchief tied round her head.

" Me and a visitor," said Mrs. Stack. " It's Mr. Morven, Miss Hardy." She performed the introduction with a flustered air, gazing at her hands first on one side and then on the other as she always did when she felt ill at ease.

Kate Hardy did not say they had already met. She smiled rather mischievously and shook hands with her visitor. " How nice of you to come," she said. " I've just made coffee. I hope you like coffee, Mr. Morven."

" Very much, thank you," said Richard gravely.

Mrs. Stack left them to it. She took off her coat and hung it on a nail behind the door ; she took her apron out of her basket, shook it out and put it on. She seemed very much at home in the Dower House kitchen, and Richard remembered that she had been friends with Aunt Ellen's cook.

Kate had abandoned work and was sitting on the table, which was the only piece of furniture in the room. She said, " The more I see of this house the more I wonder how you could bear to sell it, Mr. Morven."

" I needed the money," replied Richard. " Now that the war is over there are all sorts of things to be done. For instance, Mrs. Stack wants a new gate."

" Oh, Mr. Morven ! " cried Mrs. Stack in horror-stricken tones. " Oh, sir, how can you ! I said Walter would do it, and so he will . . ." She hesitated and then began to laugh. " Well, there now," she said. " I *am* silly. Slow on the uptake, that's what Mary says. Of course it was just Mr. Morven's fun. He could give me half a dozen gates without noticing."

"But you'd rather have one made by Walter," said Richard, smiling at her.

Mrs. Stack was too busy to reply. She set out cups and fetched the pot of coffee and a jug of milk from the scullery. Kate and her guest sat on the kitchen table and resumed their conversation of Saturday night—or, to be accurate, Sunday morning.

"What kind of books?" asked Richard. (There was no need to worry about Mrs. Stack. She came and went. She was perfectly happy and the last thing she wanted was to be included in the conversation.)

Kate did not reply at once. She was pouring out the coffee.

"I've been wondering ever since," continued Richard. "Perhaps you left that interesting announcement to the last moment so that you could shut the door upon impertinent inquiries."

"Not impertinent inquiries," she said, taking the question seriously. "People have to assume an interest which they may not feel. It protected us both from embarrassment."

"But I was really interested. I've been puzzling my brain for two days trying to remember an author called Kate Hardy."

"Why?"

"So that I could buy her books."

"An admirable reason!" exclaimed Kate, laughing. "What author could resist such a plea? And yet I feel a little reluctant—supposing you didn't like my books! Think of that, Mr. Morven! Wouldn't that be an uncomfortable position for you—an author at your very door whose books you despised!"

"I'll take the risk. It's a very small risk, Miss Hardy."

"But should I take the risk? How uncomfortable for me if I couldn't depend upon my next-door neighbour for praise and encouragement!"

Mrs. Stack had settled down to give the gas-cooker a good cleaning. She seemed completely absorbed in her task ; and even if she had wanted to listen it was doubtful if she would have understood.

"I shall find out somehow," threatened Richard.

"How, I wonder," said Kate in a thoughtful tone.

"I have a friend at Hatchard's who knows everything."

"That *is* nice for you ! "

"You're adamant ? "

"Absolutely. You see, if I don't tell you myself we can always pretend you don't know, can't we ? "

Kate was smiling as she accompanied her guest to the door and saw him walk away. They parted with cordiality and made arrangements to meet when Kate returned to Old Quinings ; but Kate was aware that beneath his apparent good humour he was slightly nettled and this amused her. Mr. Morven was used to having his own way, so it was good for him to be thwarted occasionally.

What she had told him of her feelings happened to be true. She disliked putting her friends to the trouble of praising her work whether they wanted to or not. If she had said to Mr. Morven, "I write as Kenneth Hardy," he would have felt bound to exclaim with rapture that he was enchanted with Kenneth Hardy's novels. It might be true that he liked them—a great many people did—but that sort of praise was no good and Kate preferred to do without it. She was not in the least ashamed of her work ; she had no cause to be ashamed, for she put the best of herself into her books and her sales were more than satisfactory. This at least showed that her books gave pleasure to many people besides herself. She wrote under an assumed name because her stories were stirring and adventurous, the sort of stories one would expect from a man. They were adventure stories with a difference. There was shrewd characterisation in them and bubbling humour ; they were full of vigour and bounded along gaily from start to finish. They were well planned and well written—Kate spared no trouble to make them so. Up to date she had written three novels, each more successful than the last ; each complete in itself with an entirely separate set of characters—except for Stephen

Slade. Stephen was the link which bound the stories together so that they were known as the Slade Books and sold as such by every bookseller in the Kingdom and by many in other parts of the world. To Kate, Stephen Slade was as real as Richard Morven ; he was alive and human and vulnerable. This was why he was so popular, of course, for real people like to read about real people and prefer a man of flesh and blood with human feelings—and failings —to a puppet who can do no wrong.

CHAPTER FIVE

KATE PUT the key in the door of her flat, opened the door and went in. She went in quietly, for there was a light in the sitting-room and she wanted to see Martha Body first. Martha was in the kitchen, baking little gingerbread cakes. She took a tray of them out of the oven and laid it on the table.

" So there you are ! " said Martha grimly.

Martha was a tall gaunt Scotswoman with greying hair and strong features. Some of Kate's friends had nicknamed her the Grenadier, others called her the Bodyguard . . . there was certainly a stern and forbidding aspect about Martha Body as she stood and looked at Kate with her arms folded across her chest ; but Kate, knowing her, was not alarmed.

" Yes, here I am," agreed Kate with a cheerful smile. " You got my letter all right, Martha."

" I found a wee note in the tea-caddy," said Martha in disgust. " It said you'd be away for a week and I needn't worry myself. I'd like to know why you wanted to rush away like that without telling me a word about it, Miss Kate. You could have knocked me down with a feather when I got back from the shops and you'd gone. You forgot your bedroom slippers, too."

" I know," said Kate. " The fact is I packed in a hurry."

"Mrs. Dove has been in a fine way. I've had an awful time with her."

"Perhaps I shouldn't have done it," said Kate with a sigh. She sat down at the table as she spoke, and taking one of the little cakes off the tray began to eat it.

"Why shouldn't you?" demanded Martha, changing her tune. "There's no need to ask permission from Mrs. Dove if you want to spend a week with your friends."

"I went to the country," said Kate. "How would you like to live in the country, Martha?"

"Live in the country?"

"Yes, would you like it? There wouldn't be any smuts."

"There's worse things than smuts, Miss Kate. The truth is I'm used to smuts. I doubt you'd find it a bit dull in the country, and houses are hard to get."

"I've bought a house," admitted Kate.

Martha stood and stared for a few moments without speaking. Then she said, "Well, if you've bought it that's settled."

"Yes," said Kate doubtfully. "Yes, it's settled. I hoped you'd be pleased."

Martha hesitated and then said, "I know somebody who'll not be pleased, but there's no need for us to worry ourselves about that. If we want to live in the country we'll live there."

Kate helped herself to another little cake. "I think you'll like it," she said. "It's a lovely house, Martha. I'm having it cleaned. I can get the furniture out of store and have it sent down next week."

"We're not letting the grass grow under our feet," said Martha dryly. "There'll be a fine old row when you tell Mrs. Dove, I warn you."

"It's a little hard on them, perhaps."

"Hard on them!" cried Martha Body indignantly. "It's time they had something hard. Miss Minta is not so bad, but Mrs. Dove thinks the whole place belongs to her; I can tell you it makes my blood boil sometimes the way she speaks to you, Miss Kate—and you paying for everything and treating her like a queen. Where's her gratitude, that's what I want to know."

" I don't want gratitude, Martha."

" No, you don't want it, but they ought to have it. There's something wrong with people who take everything and haven't got a spark of gratitude in them."

Kate pondered. She knew it was true (so many of Martha's trenchant remarks were true). She didn't want the gratitude of Milly and Minta but they ought to feel it. They ought to make an effort to give something in return —even if it were only a little consideration. Kate worked hard and paid for everything and they accepted it all as their due. They lived in comfort but they did not enjoy it. They grumbled about the food and criticised Martha's cooking and blamed Kate for anything that went wrong. It was funny when you thought of it like that.

" The fact is," said Kate, smiling and helping herself to another cake. " The fact is I began to feel I couldn't bear it any longer. That's the real truth, Martha."

Martha was stirring a pot on the fire. She looked over her shoulder and said, " You'll make yourself sick if you eat all those cookies straight out of the oven, Miss Kate."

" I like them like that," replied Kate. " Of course I shall keep on the flat, you know. I couldn't turn them into the street."

" No," agreed Martha. She smiled grimly and added, " But how they'll manage, dear knows. It takes me all my time to keep the place tidy, running after them all day long and cleaning up their rooms. I'd like to see this flat when they've been here a week by themselves."

" You wouldn't like to see it."

" Maybe you're right."

" You'll like the Dower House. I know you will."

" It's to be hoped so," said Martha. " We'll be on our own, anyway. It'll be like old times when the war was on."

" But without the bombs, Martha."

"It was a deal more peaceful, to my mind—bombs and all. Just you and me, Miss Kate."

"Just you and me," agreed Kate, smiling.

After this eminently satisfactory interview Kate went into the sitting-room and found Milly sitting by the fire with a book. Milly was fair and fluffy (a complete contrast to Kate). She had always been considered the pretty Miss Hardy and in consequence had been thoroughly spoilt. Her husband had spoilt her too, and when he died Milly looked round for somebody else who would take on the good work, and protect her from trouble and annoyance. Kate was the only person available and to tell the truth Kate had done pretty well. Milly was eight years older than Kate but she did not look it. She had had an easy life.

"I'm back," said Kate, taking up the poker and re-arranging the fire. "I hope you didn't worry about me. I decided to go quite suddenly. You got my note, I hope."

"Of course I was worried," declared Milly. "It was most inconsiderate of you to tear off like that without telling me a word about it. Where on earth did you go? I rang up the Clarksons but you weren't there." She raised her large brown eyes and looked at Kate questioningly. "You look——" said Milly in sudden surprise. "You look as if you had had a good time!"

Kate laughed. "I've had a marvellous time," she declared. "Simply marvellous, but, for all that, perfectly respectable."

"Kate! What a way to talk. As if I should ever think——"

"You had your suspicions," laughed Kate. "I don't blame you in the least. Why shouldn't you think what you like? Why shouldn't I do as I like for that matter?"

"You shouldn't talk like that," said Milly primly. "I know you, of course, but any one who didn't know you would be horrified. You're getting rather—rather peculiar, Kate. You talk in that wild sort of way and you're some-times a little bit inconsiderate and selfish about things. I've noticed it particularly just lately, so I thought I'd tell you—it's a pity to let that sort of thing *grow* on you."

Kate was so taken aback that she could not speak.

" Minta has noticed it too," continued Milly in gentle reproach. " We were talking it over together and we decided I ought to tell you. I don't like telling you, of course."

" It hurts you more than it hurts me, I suppose," said Kate, finding her voice. A few moments ago she had felt sorry for Milly (Milly had looked rather pathetic, sitting alone by the fire), but now Kate's feelings had changed, she was annoyed.

" Oh, Kate, I hoped you would take it *sensibly*," complained Milly. " Minta and I were amazed at your going off like that, and you haven't even told me where you've been. You can't say *that's* very considerate."

" I bought a house and I went to inspect my property," replied Kate. " It's at Old Quinings—not far from Wandlebury—in the depths of the country."

" Kate ! " exclaimed Milly in horror-stricken tones. " You don't mean—you can't mean——" she swallowed. " It's just a week-end cottage, of course, isn't it ? "

" I'm going to live there, Milly."

" Live there ! Live in the depths of the country ! You must have gone mad ! "

" I've gone sane," said Kate gravely. " It's a beautiful place, so quiet and peaceful. I shall have time to write—and think—all the time in the world."

" But why ? Why this sudden idea ? " cried Milly in a harsh voice. " It's mad to leave London now, when the war's over and every one is coming back. Why didn't you consult *me* before you dashed in and bought the place ? It's so *like* you, so impulsive, so rash ! I could have advised you about it ; we could have talked it over—all three of us together. Surely Minta and I had a right to be consulted—or do you think you have the right to settle our lives for us ? "

" I think I have the right to settle my own life," said Kate quite gently.

Milly gasped.

"If you don't want to live at Old Quinings you needn't," continued Kate. "There's no reason why you should. I want to live there—that's definite."

"Oh, Kate!" wailed Milly. "Oh, Kate, I never thought you could be so selfish! I can't think what's come over you. Minta and I came to live with you so that you shouldn't be lonely all by yourself, and now, all of a sudden, you spring this upon us out of the blue. You break up everything just for a sudden whim. You'll be *miserable* in the country all by yourself. I know you will." She hesitated for a moment and then said in a different tone, "Think it over, Kate. You can easily sell the house, can't you? We're so happy and comfortable together . . . please, Kate."

Kate was silent. She had expected reproaches and pleas, and had decided that she must be hard-hearted. It was because Kate knew her own weaknesses where Milly was concerned (and because she hated scenes and would do anything, or almost anything, for peace) that she had bought the house first and told Milly afterwards. She had burnt her boats—but that was the wrong metaphor, thought Kate; no boats were burnt. She had bought her boat, the boat in which she intended to sail away to a completely new life.

"You aren't listening!" cried Milly furiously. "You sit there smiling in that idiotic way! You might at least *listen* to me . . . this is a frightful shock; I feel quite ill. What do you propose Minta and I should *do*?"

"If you and Minta want to stay here I'll keep on the flat for you," offered Kate.

"It's the *least* you can do," declared Milly. "You can't turn us out into the street. I'm sure I don't know how we shall manage without any help . . . would Martha stay, I wonder? You can always get maids in the country quite easily, Kate."

"Why not ask Martha?" suggested Kate, hiding a smile.

"I shall," said Milly, nodding.

Kate felt that on the whole she had got off lightly. She rose and said, " There will be just time for me to have a bath before supper. Why don't you have a glass of sherry ? It will do you good."

" But we haven't *discussed* it ! " cried Milly. " We must discuss it *thoroughly*. It isn't *settled*. You can't really *want* to leave town ! " and the whole argument began again—or at least Milly's side of it. Kate had said all she intended and there was nothing she disliked more than a re-cooked dish. She was therefore quite pleased when they were interrupted by Minta, who burst into the room in her usual breezy fashion and threw her badminton racket onto a chair.

" Hallo, you're back ! " she exclaimed. " Mother has been in the most awful flap about you. Where on earth have you been ? "

" In the country," replied Kate. " As a matter of fact——"

" Rather you than me," interrupted Minta. " The country is a wash-out as far as I'm concerned—not that there's much to do in town, either. This afternoon was an absolute frost ; nothing but rabbits. We didn't have a single decent four."

" You're late, darling," said Milly.

" I know," replied Minta, taking a comb out of her bag and running it through her curls. " I meant to be early, but Billy said he'd run me home in his car and of course we had to stop for a drink. The amount of liquid refreshment that man needs is positively staggering."

(It was curious how history repeated itself, thought Kate, reminded of another daughter who had come home later than usual because she had been " seen home " by a young man. This mother was less wise, however.)

" Oh, darling, how thrilling ! " cried Milly. " Billy is absolutely crazy about you—any one can see that—and he's got a marvellous car, hasn't he ? "

" I'm going to have my bath," said Kate, walking to the door.

"Oh, you can't, Aunt Kate," objected Minta. "I'm having a bath before supper and there won't be enough hot water for us both. You can have yours later."

"Thank you, Minta," said Kate with sarcasm.

"But honestly I *want* a bath," explained Minta, raising her eyebrows. "You know quite well I always like a bath after badminton, so how you can have thought——"

"Minta!" interrupted Milly, making signs to her.

"What?" said Minta. "What on earth's the matter? Oh, damn! All right, then, I suppose you had better have it if you want, but I must say it's rather selfish of you, Aunt Kate. You haven't been playing badminton all the afternoon. The fact is," continued Minta in an aggrieved tone of voice, "the fact is it's a most frightful nuisance only having enough water for one hot bath at a time. We ought to move into a better flat—that's what I think."

"Minta!" cried Milly, signalling wildly.

"But you think so, too," said Minta in surprise. "You said so only the other day when we were discussing it. This flat is too poky for the three of us and Martha; there literally isn't room to turn."

Kate was really quite sorry for Milly. She was crimson in the face, she looked as if she were going to burst.

"Minta, I'm sure I never——" she began.

"Shut up, Ma," said her daughter in dulcet tones. "What's the good of beating about the bush? You said yourself that we ought to move—and so we should. My room is an absolute hovel; I haven't half enough space to hang my frocks . . . Martha's room is a good deal better, of course," she added with sudden inspiration, and she looked at her aunt in a hopeful manner as she spoke.

"You can move into it next week," said Kate briskly. "I'm going to have my bath now. I think your mother wants to talk to you about something, Minta."

It was a most unpleasant week. There were tears and reproaches from Milly and sulks from Minta. ("It's a surprise to find we're so popular, Miss Kate," remarked

Martha Body with her usual dry humour.) The fact was both Milly and Minta had begun to realise how comfortable they had been in the past and how much less comfortable they would be in the future. There would be no Martha to queue for rations, to cook and scrub and do all the work. There would be no Kate to look after the hundred and one small matters connected with the flat, to provide theatre tickets and taxis and new frocks. Milly had some money of her own ; quite enough to live on comfortably if she got the flat rent free, but not enough to throw about in free-handed extravagance. Besides, Milly was a trifle stingy and preferred to enjoy herself at other people's expense rather than pay for her own and her daughter's food and clothing and entertainment out of her own purse. Milly did not mention this, of course ; her objections to Kate's departure were on a much higher plane. She and Kate were sisters ; they had no other relations in the world. They were perfectly happy together, weren't they ? They had had good fun together, hadn't they ? Did Kate realise that she and Minta had given up everything to come and live with her, and now they were being left in the lurch ?

Kate certainly had not realised this. Her impression of the matter was entirely different. Milly and Minta had spent the war in a poky little hotel in Wales ; Kate's impression was that she had rescued them from a situation which had become unbearable.

When Milly saw that this would not work she started on another tack. " I'm soft with Minta," declared Milly. " I know I'm too soft, but I can't help it because she's all I've got. She needs somebody like you to guide her. If you won't stay for my sake—because I ask you—you might stay for Minta's sake. Minta needs you."

This line of attack worried Kate a good deal—it was perfectly true that Minta needed a firm hand—but she hardened her heart and reminded herself that she was useless to Minta because Milly allowed nobody to criticise her, to find fault with her nor give her any sensible advice. As long as Milly was there Minta would do exactly as she liked. When Milly was not there Minta was a different person—quite a nice person, her aunt thought.

It was a dreadful week. Kate was miserable ; she might have given in to Milly's pleadings if it had not been for the mental picture she carried in her mind : the picture of the Dower House, set amongst trees with its smooth green lawn and its air of dignity and peace.

The furniture was another grievance to Milly. It had belonged to their parents and had been left to Kate. It was quite natural that it should have been left to Kate because Milly was married and comfortably settled in a house of her own. Milly had never wanted the furniture and had forgotten all about it, but now she declared that half of it should be hers. Kate spent a sleepless night wondering whether she ought to share it with Molly and in the morning she went along to her lawyer and explained the case to him.

" She hasn't a leg to stand on," said Mr. Chester firmly. " The furniture was left to you unconditionally."

" I know," agreed Kate. " I know it's mine legally, but is it perfectly fair ? The furniture belonged to our parents . . . the fact is I don't feel very comfortable about it."

" I see," said Mr. Chester, nodding. " Yes, I see. But if I remember rightly Mrs. Dove received a sum of money in lieu. If she wants a share of the furniture, and if you are prepared to be generous in the matter, she would have to refund that sum and also half the cost of storage. The furniture was stored for ten years and the cost has been considerable. I can give you the exact figure, of course. I rather think," said Mr. Chester with a complacent air, " I rather think that will settle the matter."

Kate thought so too. " ' A Daniel come to judgment,' " she declared.

" From the *Merchant of Venice*, I believe," said Mr. Chester, who liked to show his literary client that he was not altogether an ignoramus where literary matters were concerned.

Kate said she believed it was, and they parted with expressions of mutual esteem.

CHAPTER SIX

IT HAD RAINED all day and the evening closed in early, dark and gloomy for the time of year. Kate was quite pleased that this was so, for she was tired and it was very restful with the curtains drawn across the french windows and the fire burning cosily in the grate. She sat on the sofa near the fire, knitting a pullover for Minta's birthday, but every now and then she put down her work and looked round. It was nice to see the furniture again ; she remembered it all so well. Every piece was an old friend, and Kate had a feeling that her old friends were happy to be in use again and comfortable in their new surroundings. Some of the pieces were shabby and worn but there was nothing shoddy about them. It was good old-fashioned stuff and suited the Dower House remarkably well. The place looked a trifle bare, of course, for the rooms were large and airy, but Kate did not mind that, it gave one a feeling of space.

The clocks ticked, the cupboards creaked and the log shifted with a rustle on its bed of red-hot ashes. Kate's needles clicked industriously for a few minutes and then they stopped. She rose and went to the window and pulled the curtain aside . . . How lovely it was to think it did not matter now ! The war had been over for a long time but it still gave Kate a pleasure to show a " chink." It might not be real peace yet, thought Kate, pulling back the curtain so that the chink increased to a beam, but at least you could let your light shine before men.

It was a very dark night but quite warm. Kate stepped out of the french windows and let the curtains close behind her. How dark it was ! So dark that the air felt like black plush, soft and thick against her skin—a tangible darkness— and the silence was tangible too. The silence was positive and not merely the negation of sound. Darkness and silence were country things. In town there was always a glimmer

of light somewhere and a murmur of sound. Until to-night
Kate had not known what darkness and silence meant. She
knew now. There was magic in it ; there was something a
little frightening in it. She stood and breathed the air . . .
the air felt heavier, thicker ; there was a smell of wet earth
which was part of the magic. Magic, thought Kate. Yes,
there was magic here. You could imagine all sorts of queer
things happening on a night like this . . . in a place like
this.

Having worked herself up with thoughts of strange
happenings, Kate was startled to see a tiny spot of light, a
glowing pin-point, appear quite suddenly in the dark. It
approached in an erratic sort of way, moving up and down
and backwards and forwards as it came . . . and then she
heard the crunch of footsteps on the path and smelt the
unmistakable fragrance of a cigar.

Kate pulled the curtain aside ; the light, shining out,
revealed Richard Morven.

" I had no idea you were there ! " exclaimed Richard
with a gasp of surprise. " It's as dark as the inside of a box.
I kept on bumping into trees and wished at least a dozen
times that I had had the sense to bring a torch, but I know
the path so well that I never even thought of it."

" Come in," said Kate hospitably. " I'm more or less
settled now."

Richard came in and stood on the hearthrug before the
fire. He said, " I'm sorry to disobey orders but I can't help
it. Stephen Slade happens to be one of my greatest friends."

Kate did not reply at once ; she busied herself arranging
the curtains. " You see how it is ! " she said at last. " I
just simply don't know how one should reply to that sort of
thing. I'm pleased, of course, that goes without saying, but
I can't take it graciously."

" You ought to be proud."

" I *am* proud, you silly man. That's just why ! " exclaimed Kate, laughing.

Richard laughed too. " You aren't going to throw me
into the outer darkness ? "

" Not if you behave properly," replied Kate.

She came over to the fire and once more he was struck by the way she moved, by her awkward grace ; she strode, she sat down with a quick swirl, she rose all of a piece like an unfolding spring. She did not think of movement and translate her thought into action ; as she was unconscious of her body as a young colt.

Kate stood for a moment, looking at her guest and smiling. Then, indicating that he should take a chair, she subsided upon the hearthrug in front of the fire ; subsided suddenly, as if she had no bones. He had seen the phenomenon before, of course.

They talked. Richard wanted to know all that had happened, and how she had got on with her move. She gave him an expurgated account of her week in town. Milly and Minta were presented in a becoming light—for Kate was not given to telling tales out of school—but it was quite a funny story all the same.

" I must see the Bodyguard," declared Richard at last.

" You shall," nodded Kate. " But first there's something I want to ask you. It's something that puzzled me—it's a mystery. What does this mean ?" She made the gesture which had amused Abijah Rannish, the gesture of taking handfuls of chaff and throwing them into the air.

There was a moment's silence and then Richard said in a strangely sharp voice, " Where on earth did you see that ? "

" It's something—horrible ? "

" You actually saw people doing that, Miss Hardy ? "

" No," she replied. " Not really. I did it myself."

" Tell me about it," he said.

Kate told him.

" It was absolutely ridiculous, of course," she admitted with a deprecating smile. " One does these ridiculous things without thinking—at least I do. I suppose Abijah took me for a lunatic."

" Not a lunatic," said Richard gravely. " He took you for a witch."

" A witch ! Goodness, how amusing ! Do you mean to say there are witches in Old Quinings—what fun ! "

Richard did not smile. He said, " Abijah thought you were a ' scatterer.' That's what they call them in this part of the country. It's safer not to speak of witches. The motions of bending and picking up handfuls of chaff and throwing them into the air is ' scattering.' I'm sorry Abijah saw you."

" Does it matter ? "

" No, of course not," replied Richard too hastily. " But I had hoped people had forgotten all that long ago. It appears they haven't. And Abijah is a particularly nasty specimen of the genus *homo sapiens*. I had the most frightful trouble with him only the other day, it was most unpleasant —he went off grumbling and growling and vowing vengeance."

Kate was completely baffled. She saw that her guest took the subject of witches seriously, but witches were creatures out of fairy-tales : you saw them in children's plays dressed in red cloaks and black hats ; they rode on broomsticks with black cats sitting beside them ; they stirred cauldrons full of nauseous herbs and chanted spells.

" You do understand, don't you ? " said Kate suddenly. " It was just sheer silliness on my part."

He smiled and said he understood ; and so he did. It was in keeping with his ideas about her ; she had felt happy and her feeling had been expressed immediately in action . . . it was unfortunate that her action had taken that particular form. He wondered why. Was there some deep significance in the action ? Was it a relic from the days when happy people felt the urge to propitiate their gods by gifts of corn ? And if so, why should it possess that other, that sinister significance ?

" Don't talk about it to any one," said Richard after a few moments' silence. " Take my advice and walk delicately until you begin to understand. There are odd things in Old Quinings—queer things. Leave them alone, Miss Hardy."

" But the people seem so friendly, so—so wholesome and sensible."

" Some of them are."

" Mrs. Stack, for instance."

" Ah, Mrs. Stack ! " exclaimed Richard with a smile. " Mrs. Stack and Mrs. Rogers, the Turners and the Grays . . . there you have the best. At the other end of the social scale you have people like Rannish and his granddaughter, incredibly dirty and thriftless and practically illiterate. Between these two poles there are at least half a dozen grades of society. You might not notice the difference—it seems slight to us—but the difference is there."

" Socialism is unknown in Old Quinings ? "

" I wouldn't say that. There is socialism here as in other places, but it doesn't seem to work in Old Quinings. I can't explain it to you ; I'm merely stating a plain fact. There *are* these different social planes in the village, quite separate and distinct. People from one plane may mix with those from another, but they do so with their eyes open ; they know their own status and accept the position as unalterable. It's an example of realism."

" Six grades between Mrs. Stack and Abijah ? "

" That shouldn't surprise you. There's an unbridgable gulf between them. Mrs. Stack and Abijah are far further apart than—well, than the King and myself," declared Richard, smiling. " If the King and I were to meet upon a desert island I feel sure we should have quite a lot in common —we could be companions—whereas Mrs. Stack and Abijah would have nothing in common at all. They are so utterly different that they might be a different species of animal."

They both laughed, and Kate, seizing upon the idea, began to suggest all sorts of fantastic situations which would be bound to arise upon a desert island inhabited by such oddly assorted couples. Richard was intensely amused, he was also intensely interested ; here he saw for a few brief moments the creator of his friend, Stephen Slade.

They were thus engaged when the door opened and Martha Body came in with the coffee tray.

"Oh, Martha, what a good idea!" exclaimed Kate. "This is Mr. Morven, the former owner of the house."

"Good evening, Miss Body," said Richard, accepting the introduction in a friendly manner.

"Good evening, sir," returned Martha brusquely as she set down the tray.

"Will you please bring another cup—for Mr. Morven," said Kate. "Mr. Morven likes coffee, as I happen to know."

"That cup's for him, Miss Kate."

"What?" said Kate. "Oh, Martha, what nonsense!"

"It's not nonsense, Miss Kate. You know as well as I do if you take coffee at this hour you'll never sleep. I'll bring in your usual gruel when the gentleman has gone." And so saying, Martha went out and shut the door firmly.

"You see what I have to endure!" exclaimed Kate, half laughing and half annoyed.

"She's quite right. I've stayed too long," said Richard, rising. "She's an excellent Bodyguard—I take off my hat to her! No, I won't have coffee, thank you. It keeps me awake, too."

When her guest had gone Kate went into the kitchen and had her gruel sitting by the fire with Martha. It had become a habit and they both enjoyed a chat before they went to bed.

"He seemed a nice enough gentleman," Martha said. "Mrs. Stack was talking about him this morning. She thinks the world of him."

Mrs. Stack came in daily to help Martha and her views and opinions were frequently quoted to Kate. The two women got on very well together (Kate had hoped they would, but you never could tell with Martha, she was a law unto herself).

"Mrs. Stack says his wife is in America," continued Martha. "You'll know about that, no doubt?"

"He told me," said Kate.

"M'phm," said Martha, nodding. "To my mind a man's not a proper man if he can't keep his wife in order."

CHAPTER SEVEN

IT WAS now May and Old Quinings lay buried in drifts of snowy blossoms. Not only the Morven orchard (which was a sight that drew visitors from all over the country) but the whole village blossomed and burgeoned in the warm spring sunshine. The village green was dotted with fruit trees, and even the smallest cottage garden had its cherry or apple or pear. Old Quinings was fruit-minded. Every one knew about fruit, talked about it seriously and ate it with critical appreciation in Old Quinings.

Kate had been settled in Dower House for over a month. She had met Miss Crease, of course. The Vicar's wife, Mrs. Barton, had called. Miss Carlyle, who taught at the village school, had spoken to Kate in the grocer's shop and introduced herself. She was about Kate's age; a neat little woman with fair fluffy hair and bright blue eyes. There was something attractive about Miss Carlyle and Kate had a feeling that they would have a good deal in common. At present Kate was too busy to do much about it, but she promised herself that one of these days when she had time to breathe she would ring up Miss Carlyle and ask her to tea.

The house was fairly straight by this time, or at least as straight as Kate and Martha could get it, but there was a lot to be done in the way of repairs, and try as she might Kate could not get a workman for this purpose. Mr. Seager, the village carpenter, had promised to come himself or to send one of his men as soon as he could manage it; meantime they had to carry on as best they could with broken sash-cords and doors which had sagged on their hinges and would neither open nor shut.

The garden was in an even worse condition and was disimproving daily. Weeds were springing up unchecked, hedges needed trimming and the vegetable plot lay fallow. It seemed impossible to get a gardener to tackle the job.

Mrs. Barton had suggested that Kate should tackle the job herself; she had seemed to think there was little difficulty about it; but Kate knew nothing about gardens and did not know where to start. Besides, it was high time Kate began her fourth novel, and once she got her teeth into that she would have no energy to spare for her garden. Martha was of the opinion that Miss Kate should wait a little and enjoy herself before starting another book. But Martha didn't understand—another story featuring Stephen Slade was already taking shape in Kate's mind, and what was the use of coming to the country for peace to write and not making use of the amenity?

Having asked herself this question, Kate answered it by laying in a large stock of paper and starting work forthwith. She wrote daily in the morning-room with the sun shining in at the open french windows and the birds singing gaily in the trees outside. These were delightful accompaniments to the labour of composition and the author appreciated them accordingly; she also appreciated the efforts of Martha and Mrs. Stack, who ran the house together and protected her from interruption.

The IDEA which had visited Kate in the barn and which she had likened to a fawn bounding through the thicket, returned to her as she had known it would and was now being tamed. Kate was treating it very carefully, not hurrying it at all, but coaxing it with unlimited patience to feed out of her hand. It was good. She knew that. She was beginning to suspect it was very good indeed. There were set-backs, of course. Some days things wouldn't come right—the fawn was intractable—but other days she made excellent progress and all went well.

This was one of the good days. Kate had got Stephen moving, she had steered him round an awkward corner, which had bothered her considerably, and everything was working out in the pleasantest way imaginable. Her pencil was racing over the paper, leaving gaps here and there to be filled in at leisure. She was so absorbed that she did not hear the door open, but after a few moments she became aware that someone was standing beside her. Raising her eyes in a dazed sort of manner she beheld Mrs. Stack.

"Oh, Miss Hardy!" said Mrs. Stack in a trembling voice. "I know you're writing (and what Miss Body would say I'm sure I don't know), but I had to see you for a minute. Walter's coming." She held out a telegram form as she spoke.

Kate took it and read : *Arriving this afternoon don't trouble to meet love Walter.*

"Of course you must go," said Kate, abandoning Stephen reluctantly. "You won't meet him, of course, because he doesn't want you to. He wants to find you in the Lodge when he comes home. How lovely for you, Mrs. Stack ! How exciting ! "

"Yes, of course," said Mrs. Stack doubtfully. She looked upset—which was perhaps natural—but the emotion she was trying to hide was not joy.

"After all these years," said Kate encouragingly.

"Yes," nodded Mrs. Stack still more doubtfully.

"You're so proud of Walter, aren't you ? "

"Oh, yes, of course I am ! " cried Mrs. Stack. This was absolutely definite.

"Well, then, why——" began Kate and paused uncertainly.

Mrs. Stack was looking down at her hands, turning them first one way and then the other and gazing at them as if she had never seen them before and did not like the look of them very much. "I don't know," she said in a low voice. "I'm wondering. I mean, will Walter be happy ? "

"Happy ! Of course he'll be happy. He's been longing to get home."

"That's why," said Mrs. Stack.

They were silent, looking at one another.

"You see," said Mrs. Stack at last, "you see it's seven years since Walter went away. That's a long time, isn't it ? We've stayed the same but he's changed—well, that goes without saying, doesn't it, Miss ? Of course he's changed. He's an officer."

" He's still Walter, your son."

" Yes, he's a good boy—always was—but he's used to different things and different sort of people. I can tell he's changed by his letters—wonderful letters they are. Of course I'm pleased he's coming, but supposing he's disappointed."

" He won't be——" Kate began, and then she paused. Mrs. Stack was looking at her questioningly, not wanting facile comfort and assurances, wanting sympathy and understanding. " I don't know Walter," said Kate thoughtfully. " If I knew him I might be able to tell you better. I understand exactly what you feel but I think you should trust Walter."

" Oh, I *do* ! " exclaimed Mrs. Stack. " I could always trust Walter ! "

" You aren't trusting him," Kate pointed out. " You think he's forgotten you."

" No, Miss. I know he hasn't forgotten us (he's always writing and sending me little presents ; he's a good son, Walter is), but I think he's seeing me and Mary and the Lodge Cottage in a sort of dream. I think he's been dreaming about his home all these years and remembering all the nice things about it. He's changed—but he doesn't know he's changed. That's what I think."

" It will be exciting for him to get home and see all his old haunts," declared Kate.

" Just at first, perhaps, but what about afterwards ? I wrote and said to him I thought he should come for a bit—not stay here—but Walter says no, he's coming home to stay and he's going to take on his old job again. He was with Mr. Seager before the war, and of course Mr. Seager will be glad to get him ; he always says Walter was one of his best workmen."

Kate put her elbow on the desk, and, chin in hand, gazed out of the window ; she was trying to put herself into Walter's shoes. At last she said, " I can only say again you must trust him. Welcome him warmly—well, of course you'll do that—and be yourself. Be absolutely natural. If Walter isn't happy here he must go elsewhere, but obviously he thinks he'll be happy."

" I don't want him to be disappointed," said Mrs. Stack pitifully.

" You're little house is charming," said Kate. " You and Mary are perfect dears—how could he be disappointed ? "

" There won't be much scope for him," declared Mrs. Stack, uncomforted. " I can't see him making window-frames and mending roofs all day and going down to the Bull and Bush and playing darts with the village boys—not after all he's done and all the people he's met and all the wonderful things he's seen."

Kate couldn't either.

" As for being natural, like you said," continued Mrs. Stack, almost in tears, " as for being natural—well, I don't see how I can—somehow. I don't feel as if I would know—what to say——"

" Would you like to bring him to supper ? " said Kate impulsively.

" Here, Miss ! " exclaimed Mrs. Stack in amazement.

" Yes, of course. Would you like to bring him to-night and we'll have a ' Welcome Home ' party—you and I and Mary and Walter ? Would you like it ? "

" Oh, Miss Hardy, that would be lovely, but—— "

" Off you go ! " said Kate, laughing and waving her away. " Go and tidy up your house for the major. Clean it thoroughly, Mrs. Stack ; you may find a speck of dust under his bed if you use a magnifying glass . . . think how frightful that would be ! Then you must put on your best frock and have the kettle boiling for tea. Oh, and don't forget the potato scones, will you ? "

" But, Miss Hardy—really—— "

" I'll expect you at eight o'clock," said Miss Hardy, seizing her pen.

Mrs. Stack went—but it was too late. The sequence of Kate's thought was broken. Stephen was lifeless—a mere puppet—it was Walter's fault, of course. What material for a story, thought Kate (laying down her useless tool and considering the problem of Walter). This must be happening all over the country ; the details varying but the essentials the same . . .

CHAPTER EIGHT

KATE determined to have a slap-up Welcome Home Party for Walter Stack. The fatted calf was killed—which is to say that she and Martha spent the whole afternoon cooking, baking and opening tins and bottles. The discovery that Martha was willing to co-operate was a relief to Kate's mind, for you never knew with Martha. She had her own ideas. She was willing to co-operate in the preparation of the feast but refused the invitation to be present, and not all Kate's blandishments could induce her to change her mind.

" I know my place, Miss Kate," said Martha firmly. " And what's more I like it. I'll be much more comfortable sitting by the kitchen fire with a nice book than sitting in the dining-room all dolled up with you and the Stacks, and talking a lot of nonsense. If Mrs. Stack likes it she can do it and welcome. I only hope she *will* like it, that's all."

" Of course she'll like it ! " cried Kate. " Why shouldn't she ? It's going to be a lovely party."

The Stacks arrived as the clock in the church tower struck eight. They left their wraps in the hall and were shown into the drawing-room, where their hostess was waiting. Mrs. Stack was in black silk with a gold chain round her neck and a large and most beautiful cameo brooch which—although its owner was unaware of the fact—was the very latest fashion. Mary had a pretty blue-flowered voile frock which became her vastly. There was a little confusion at the door as Martha ushered them in, because Mrs. Stack wished her son to precede her, and her son was unwilling to do so, but eventually Mrs. Stack was induced to lead the way and did so in a flustered manner.

"This is Walter, Miss Hardy," said Mrs. Stack, nervously regarding her hands.

Kate had seen Walter's photograph, of course, but his photograph had not prepared her for any one so vital. He was a tall man, broad-chested and strong. His head was round with thick brown hair, his eyes were widely set and very dark blue. He was not really good-looking in the usual sense of the word, but there was something very attractive about him (Kate was reminded of a picture of Drake she had seen somewhere). She had heard a good deal about Walter Stack and had formed a mental picture of him, but this man was completely different from the man she had imagined, so different that for one absurd moment Kate could not believe that this was really Walter Stack. She had expected him to be younger, to be shy and a little awkward; she had decided that she must put him at his ease, must draw him out and make friends with him; but he was not in the least shy or awkward and there was no need for any hard work. He was perfectly at ease; he spoke Kate's language and he was friendly from the start. Kate was a little ashamed of her expectations; she realised now that she had been silly and had imagined him without taking into account his history. Walter Stack had risen to field rank by his personal attainments, he had shouldered heavy responsibilities and commanded men in battle; he could not have done these things if he had been a mediocrity, and it was natural that doing these things should give him assurance and confidence in himself.

Walter was in uniform, for, as he explained, he had outgrown all his old clothes and had not had time to get new ones. His row of medals included a D.S.O. He sat in the chair by the fire smoking a cigarette, drinking a glass of sherry and talking as if he had known his hostess for years. Mrs. Stack and Mary were sitting side by side on the sofa. Mrs. Stack had refused sherry but Mary had accepted a glass . . . it was apparent from her expression that sherry was new to her and she did not like it much.

Kate was determined that Mrs. Stack and Mary should

take part in the conversation, and she did all she could to bring them in ; she dragged them in forcibly and they nodded or smiled or shook their heads but maintained silence. It was hopeless.

" We'll have supper now, shall we ? " said Kate.

She had taken a good deal of trouble over the table and it looked very festive with a bowl of spring flowers in the middle. The glass and silver sparkled and shone in the lamp-light. The dishes were on the sideboard—it was a cold supper except for the soup. Mrs. Stack and Mary were shown where to sit and told to sit down ; Walter helped his hostess to serve the food. This had seemed quite natural to Kate, but glancing at her female guests she realised that they were miserable ; it was unnatural to them to sit there and be waited on. At home Walter would have sat at the table and his mother and Mary would have served the food. Kate was annoyed with herself for making the mistake, but it was too late to rectify it.

" I thought there was rationing in England ! " exclaimed Walter as he placed a bowl of soup before his mother.

" Yes, dear, there is," said Mrs. Stack gravely.

" It doesn't look like it, I must say," Walter declared.

" Oh, but you don't understand, Major Stack ! " exclaimed Kate. " This is a very special occasion. We don't have parties every day."

" I like parties," Walter said as he sat down and unfolded his table-napkin.

Kate had been regretting her impulsive invitation ; she saw her party was going to be a complete failure (it was worse than a failure, it was a disaster, decided Kate). Her idea had been to tide the Stack family over the first evening, to have a gay party which would make them all feel happy and comfortable—she saw now that she could not do it, the thing was beyond her powers. Mrs. Stack had refused the hock-cup (which might have helped a little) and had prevented Mary from having it, shaking her head for-biddingly when Mary hesitated. Kate's party was doomed to failure where her female guests were concerned, but if

Walter was enjoying himself it was something. Walter *must* enjoy it, for it was his party. Walter *should* enjoy it, decided Kate. She abandoned her other guests and got Walter going on the subject of Burma. He had been all through the campaign and could speak with authority, he made it real to Kate. He told several stories about the Japs, some rather horrible, but others full of humour ; he drew a little map on the back of an envelope illustrating the campaign. Kate was so enthralled that she forgot her other guests. Except for the mechanical hospitality of offering them food they might not have been there at all.

" I think you know Colonel Ransome," said Walter at last. " He's my colonel—a thundering good fellow. Mrs. Ransome was in India and I stayed with them on my way home. They mentioned your name."

" Elsa and I are tremendous friends—we were at school together ! " exclaimed Kate. " This is frightfully interesting. Do tell me all about her, Major Stack. When are they coming home ? "

" They aren't coming home," replied Walter. " Colonel Ransome bought a tea garden in Assam and when he's demobbed he intends to stay and run it himself. He knows about tea and I must say it's an interesting business. As a matter of fact he offered to take me on. It was a good offer but I wasn't tempted. I told him I had a job waiting for me at home," added Walter, smiling at his mother as he spoke.

Mrs. Stack smiled back a little uncertainly. " But perhaps it would have been better, Walter," she said.

" Better ! " exclaimed Walter in amazement. " I was longing to get home. It was the one thing that kept me sane —thinking about Old Quinings. I used to dream about it quite a lot, too. When things went wrong and everything was absolutely damnable I used to think of the orchard in blossom, or sometimes of the Lodge Cottage with the row of hollyhocks in front. I used to work out the difference in time and say to myself they'll be having supper in the kitchen . . . or tea or breakfast or whatever it might be. Besides, I had promised, hadn't I, Mother ? Don't you remember? When I was going away I said to you, Don't worry, I'll come back all right. I promise faithfully I'll come back and make a home for you when the war's over."

"Yes, Walter, I remember," said his mother gravely. "But those sort of promises don't count——"

"All promises count," declared Walter, smiling at her.

"Not those sort, dear," said Mrs. Stack. "We were both upset . . . and things change."

They had finished supper by this time, so they rose from the table. Walter opened the door. Mrs. Stack looked at the table and then at Kate.

"It's a party," said Kate, smiling. "Martha will clear the table; don't worry about it."

"But Mary and I would *like* to help," said Mrs. Stack.

This was not what Kate had intended, and she was about to scout the idea when she happened to glance at Mrs. Stack. It was obvious that Mrs. Stack really wanted to wash up the dishes : she was looking at her hostess with pleading in her eyes.

"It's *quite* the wrong thing," said Kate, laughing. "But I'm sure Martha will be delighted."

"We shan't be a minute," declared Mrs. Stack with a relieved air. "You and Walter go into the drawing-room and talk. We'll come when we've finished."

Kate led the way into the drawing-room and turned on the radio. "I think there's dance music somewhere," she said, twiddling the knobs.

"Oh, yes, let's dance," said Walter eagerly.

They found the dance music, pushed back the sofa and turned up the rugs. A few moments later they were dancing —waltzing dreamily to the strains of the *Vienna Woods*.

"Old tunes are best," said Walter.

"I haven't danced for years," said Kate.

"That's difficult to believe."

"One doesn't forget."

"We danced quite a lot in India. As a matter of fact the last time I danced was with Elsa Ransome."

" How funny ! "

" Enormous affair at Government House."

" Rather different ! "

" Different but not any more enjoyable. This is *very* kind of you."

" I'm enjoying it every bit as much as you are, you know."

They danced silently after that. They were still dancing when the other two guests appeared.

" Now, don't stop," said Mrs. Stack, who seemed more cheerful after her activities with Martha in the pantry. " Don't stop whatever you do. Mary and I will be quite happy sitting here . . . what a good thing I polished the floor this morning, isn't it ? "

CHAPTER NINE

THE PULLOVER which Kate was knitting for Minta's birthday had been laid aside, half-finished, for Stephen Slade was occupying her time to the exclusion of all else.

" You'd better give it to me to finish," Martha said. " It'll never be done in time—next week, isn't it ? Are they coming down for the day ? "

Kate relinquished the pullover thankfully. She said, " I think I had better ask them for the week-end. Could you manage, Martha ? "

" Oh, I'll manage. It's you that'll have to bear the brunt. You'll not get much time for writing while they're here."

" I know, but all the same——" said Kate with a sigh. She sat down and wrote to Milly and took the letter out to the post before she could change her mind.

It was a fine evening. The shadows were lengthening across the village street. Kate lingered, enjoying the air. She had been writing all day and felt slightly dazed and muzzy. When she got back to the Dower House and pushed open the door in the wall she was surprised to see a man walking across the lawn to meet her. He was small and bent and wizened . . . she had seen him somewhere before . . . it was Abijah Rannish.

"The garden be in a proper mess," said Abijah. "Time was when the Dower 'Ouse garden wor a sight wid flowers an' such. It be in a proper mess, so it be."

Kate could not deny it.

"It wants diggin'," continued Abijah. "Wants the shrubs cuttin' back. You'd never get all that done in a month of Sundays. 'Ard work it be—too 'ard for wimmin. It's a man you want."

Kate agreed with him profoundly.

"I doan't mind takin' it on," continued Abijah. "I'd need a boy to 'elp—jus' for a start—jus' till I gets the place in proper trim. Arter that I could do it myself, easy. A good worker I be."

Kate hesitated. She did not like Abijah, and there was that incident in the barn . . . Mr. Morven had taken it so seriously . . . but it seemed ridiculous to be choosey when she needed a gardener badly and the man was willing to come.

"Carrots an' such like," said Abijah. "Peas an' beans did ought ter be in now—an' sweet peas. Good wid sweet peas I be. Good wid growin' plants."

He seemed simple and harmless, a little earthy man, but there was something odd about him and his eyes were shifty.

"A good worker I be," repeated Abijah. "Up in the marnin' an' at it constant. Not like some as only works their bare time. You be surprised 'ow quick I get it done. An' I doan't tell no tales neither."

He spoke so strangely that Kate had some difficulty in understanding him. It was not only the broad country vowels; the man seemed to have no teeth.

"Tales?" echoed Kate in perplexity.

"I doan't tell nothin' that I see," said Abijah, his eyes sliding away sideways as he spoke.

"That doesn't affect me," declared Kate, smiling. "I've

nothing to hide, so, if I decide to engage you, you can tell the whole village everything about me. I warn you it may not be very interesting. In fact I expect you would have to make up some stories if you want to hold the attention of your audience."

" I don't tell no lies, not like you," he mumbled.

" Like me ! "

" They do say as 'ow you make your livin' tellin' lies."

" Oh, I see," said Kate, smiling. " But that's rather different, isn't it ? Every one knows my stories aren't true."

" True tales be best—an' queerest," declared Abijah.

Kate had heard this sentiment before, expressed in different words. Being a novelist she did not agree with it. True stories were apt to be untidy and pointless—so Kate thought—and as for " queerest "—no, she could not believe that any true story could rival the imagined horrors of Poe.

" True stories," said Abijah nodding. " Stories about real people as lived 'ere in Old Quinings. 'Anded on, they be, an' told again. But book-larnin' an' such spiles the memory. It's cinemas an' books an' such-like trash children be 'avin' now. Us didden 'ave no school," declared Abijah proudly.

" None at all ? " asked Kate in surprise. " Do you mean you can't read or write, Abijah ? "

" Not me," he replied scornfully. " Nary word—an' all the better of it. Us 'ad work—work an' stories."

Kate nodded ; she understood that. Stories by word of mouth was the only sort of entertainment for people who could neither read nor write.

" Fine memory I 'ave," he boasted, and it seemed to Kate, who had an instinct for such things, that he was making his way laboriously to a definite point. " I doan't ferget nothin' I've 'eard. Granfer would sit in the sun 'an talk— old an' done 'e wor, but 'e 'adn't fergot nothin'. 'E 'adn't fergot what 'is granfer told 'im . . . an' 'is grandfer told 'im . . . 'underds of years of stories, an' all true."

It was a strange thought, interesting but oddly frightening ; a chain of stories stretching back into the dim and shadowy past. Stories about the people who had lived here, in this very place, whose feet had trodden upon this very earth . . . and all true.

" You better take me," said Abijah, returning to his plea with sudden and somewhat startling effect. " You woan't do better. Some woulden' come 'ere an' work, not for any money."

" Why ? " asked Kate in surprise. " Is it because you think I'm——" she paused. Richard Morven had warned her to walk delicately and not to speak of things she did not understand. " Because they're frightened of the ghost, I suppose," she said lightly.

" Ah ! " said Abijah, looking down and sideways, looking anywhere and everywhere except at Kate. " Some calls 'er that . . . Selina Morven. Walks, she does, an' weeps an' wrings 'er hands. Some 'as seen 'er wid the dagger in 'er side an' the blood runnin' down 'er white dress."

It was getting dark. Kate had not noticed until now ; but now, suddenly, the light seemed to have faded and the shadows of the trees were spreading and thickening. Quite suddenly it was gloomy and cold. Kate shivered.

" Pretty she wor," said Abijah reflectively. " There wor a pickter of 'er 'anging in the Dower 'Ouse when old Miss Morven wor there. Maybe you've seed it, Miss."

" No," said Kate.

" Pretty she wor," repeated Abijah, " but bad. Ah, Selina Morven wor *one of those*."

" Who ? " asked Kate. " What do you mean, Abijah ? "

He was silent for a few moments, shifting his feet. Then he began to speak. " *Maledico Trinitatem Sanctissimam nobilissimamque, Patrem*——"

" Stop ! " cried Kate. " Stop, that's frightfully wicked ! You can't mean they celebrated Black Mass ! How do you know ? Where did you hear those dreadful words, Abijah ? "

Abijah did not reply. He stood before her, humble, meek, earthy, but his eyes were bright and restless.

" Is that what you meant ? " asked Kate in a quiet voice.

" I told you," he said. " She wor *one of those*. It wor on the moor. The stones is there if you know where to look. That's where they took the goat an' 'eld it down an' killed it. All kinds there wor that went up the path, an' the moon shinin' bright like silver. All kinds there wor, gentle an' simple, men an' maidens—an' Selina Morven wor there." His voice had changed; it was higher, with a sing-song cadence, as if he were repeating word for word a long-remembered tale. " She wor a liddle slip of a thing wid tiny 'ands an' feet. Fair as May, wid golden 'air an' innocent lookin' wor Selina Morven, but the children ran when she passed by, an' the beasts sickened. 'Tweren't only the beasts, neither. Them as she ill-wished wor done for, their flesh rotted an' their senses failed——"

" It wasn't true ! " cried Kate. " It couldn't have been true——"

" Ah, but it wor true," declared Abijah. " She wor a scatterer, she wor. They took 'er an' tried 'er by water an' prickin'. She wor well an' truly tried. Wicked she wor an' full of guile—a wicked maiden for all 'er innocent looks ! "

Kate was silent. It was darker now, and very cold. She did not want to hear the end of the story—but she had to hear it.

" She wor to be burned," he continued. " Burned at the village green for all to see. That wor the proper end for such. But when they went to get 'er she wor dead wid a dagger in 'er side an' the blood runnin' down 'er white dress. The fire wor laid an' there worn't no lamb to be roasted."

" Who killed her ? "

" Ah," said Abijah. " 'Oo killed 'er ? That wor a mystery in Old Quinings many a long day. Them as knew 'eld their tongues. It wor perilous to know. The fire wor laid ready for burnin'—perilous it wor." He hesitated as if the old ban were still active, sealing his lips.

" Somebody killed her to save her from the fire," said Kate in hushed tones.

" It wor 'er true love," nodded Abijah. " She wor too tender to bear the fire. Them as knew, knew it was 'im an' no other that climbed in at 'er window an' stabbed 'er in the 'eart. It wor a kind death—too kind for such as 'er."

Kate was overcome by the horror of it. She could imagine the whole thing clearly—too clearly for her peace of mind. What a desperate expedient ! What a frightful choice to make ! She could imagine the young lovers clinging together in the darkness, whispering words of grief and tenderness, mingling their tears. A ray of moonlight from the open window caught the sharp edge of the weapon so that it gleamed like a white hot flame. Kate felt their agony in her own bosom . . . *his* agony as the moment came when he must drive the dagger into her heart . . .

" It wor better 'ad 'e let 'er burn," said Abijah slowly. " Dower 'Ouse wouldn't 'ave 'ad no ghost, not if she'd burned. Burning is the proper end for such."

Kate could bear no more. She left Abijah standing on the lawn and ran into the house.

CHAPTER TEN

MRS. STACK had not appeared at the Dower House for several days, not since the party, but Kate was not expecting her, for now that Walter was home she would have no time for outside work. Kate had suggested to Martha that they must find someone else, but Martha did not seem particularly anxious to have a stranger. On the fourth day, however, which happened to be a Monday, Mrs. Stack turned up in the afternoon. Kate discovered her in the pantry cleaning the silver.

" Oh, Mrs. Stack, I thought you weren't coming ! " exclaimed Kate.

" I can come if you need me, Miss," she replied. " Walter took a few days' holiday and we went to Wandlebury, but he's started work to-day, and there's nothing much to do at home so I thought I'd come. I hope it's all right. Martha said it was."

" It's perfectly all right," replied Kate. " Come whenever you can."

" You see, Miss," continued Mrs. Stack, taking up a fork and polishing it carefully, " you see it's a bit difficult —in a way. Walter doesn't want me to work, or at least not to take outside work ; he says he wants me to have an easy time now that he's got back ; but an easy time doesn't suit me. I get a bit tired if I haven't got plenty to do— besides, the money will be useful." She hesitated, for a moment and then seized the teapot and began to polish it. " You see," she said, " you see I've got Bertie, that's the difficulty."

" Bertie ? " inquired Kate.

" He's my eldest," explained Mrs. Stack. " I dare say you thought I just had Walter and Mary—well, the fact is we don't talk about Bertie very much." She put down the teapot and began to examine her hands. " I'm afraid Bertie isn't a very good boy, Miss Hardy," said his mother in a low voice. " He never was, really. He had every chance— just like Walter had—but—but he was difficult."

" I'm sorry," said Kate sympathetically.

" Always a worry, Bertie was, always in trouble—not ordinary boyish sort of trouble either. I found him a job in Wandlebury when he left school—a good job it was—but he got in with the wrong sort of companions and there was more trouble there. Then he went to London ; there seemed nothing else for it at the time, but I see now it wasn't the right thing for Bertie. He doesn't stick to things, Miss Hardy. He doesn't work. Well, no employer is going to keep a man who doesn't work properly. That's not the worst either," continued Mrs. Stack wretchedly. " If it was just laziness it wouldn't matter so much, but wherever he goes he seems to make trouble ; he's got all sorts of queer ideas, he gets up against people. You'd think to hear him talk that the whole world was set on doing him down . . . he can't see that all his bad luck comes from inside himself."

There was a little silence. Mrs. Stack took up the teapot

again. " Well, that's how it is," she said. " I thought I'd tell you, Miss."

" It was nice of you to tell me," declared Kate.

" So you see," said Mrs. Stack, " you see that's why I said the money would be useful. I like to have a little money handy—money of my very own. Bertie is my responsibility, not Walter's at all. I won't have Bertie being a drag on Walter."

Kate looked at Mrs. Stack polishing her teapot, and thought what a wonderful woman she was.

Having got this all off her chest Mrs. Stack became a good deal more cheerful. She breathed upon the teapot and polished industriously. " It's a lovely teapot," she said. " It's a pleasure to clean nice silver; it's rewarding, that's what I say."

" It certainly rewards you," replied Kate, smiling. " I shall be blinded by that teapot when I pour out my afternoon tea."

" I didn't half thank you for the party," said Mrs. Stack, changing the subject suddenly. " A lovely party it was. I don't know when I enjoyed a party so much."

Kate looked at her in surprise. For a moment she wondered whether Mrs. Stack intended the remark sarcastically, but Mrs. Stack was smiling at her in such a friendly manner that the suspicion died at birth.

" It *was* good of you," she continued. " All the bother you took with the food—and the table was beautiful, really beautiful. It was so *interesting*, too. I just said to Mary, ' You won't hear talk like that again in a hurry, Mary my girl.' It was good talk," declared Mrs. Stack. " I can't do with the sort of talk that goes on in the village—when is Mrs. Turner expecting her fourth, and why doesn't the Government do this and that and the other, and how many points you've got to give for sultanas—you get sick of it in half no time. I could have sat and listened to you and Walter all night. Walter talked well, didn't he, Miss ? "

" He did indeed," agreed Kate. She was delighted and amazed in equal measure to hear that Mrs. Stack had enjoyed the party. Perhaps the explanation lay in Mrs. Stack's last remark, which had been thrown out in such an elaborately careless manner. Mothers were strange beings, decided Kate.

She was still thinking about mothers when she sat down at her desk and took up her pen. She thought about Mrs. Stack and she thought about Milly. Could any two mothers be more different ? The one was so sensible, so sane, accepting the responsibilities of motherhood and carrying them gallantly ; the other was so foolish, so short-sighted as to her own interests and the interests of her child. One thing only they had in common : both were devoted to their offspring ; but Kate had read somewhere that earwigs were devoted mothers . . . it was a queer life altogether, thought Kate, smiling to herself.

"Mrs. Morven to see you, Miss Kate," said Martha, opening the door. "You're not too busy to see her, are you ? "

"Mrs. Morven ! You don't mean *Mrs. Morven*, Martha ! "

"Yes, Miss Kate," said Martha patiently. "I put her in the drawing-room. Very smart she is, with fully-fashioned silk stockings and patent leather shoes."

"She's come from America," explained Kate, laying down her pen and rising—and hesitating.

"She can't eat you," said Martha, holding the door open.

This was so like Martha that Kate was forced to smile, and was still smiling when she opened the drawing-room door and went in.

Mrs. Morven was sitting on the sofa. She was beautiful, there was no doubt of that. In fact she was the most beautiful creature Kate had ever seen, and because Kate loved beauty she was immediately prejudiced in Mrs. Morven's favour.

"Forgive me, Miss Hardy," said Mrs. Morven, rising. "I know you're a busy woman but I'll try not to keep you too long. I've come several thousand miles to see you."

" To see *me* ! " exclaimed Kate in surprise.

" To see *you*," nodded Mrs. Morven. " I expect you know the position—about Dickie and me, I mean."

" Yes," said Kate. " Mr. Morven told me. Do sit down, won't you ? "

" I'm glad you know," said Mrs. Morven, sitting down and crossing her long, beautiful silken legs. " That makes it a lot easier. I needn't bore you with my side of the story, Miss Hardy."

" It wouldn't bore me," Kate told her.

" What I meant was, Dickie will have told you impartially ; he would be perfectly fair—besides, I haven't got a leg to stand on. I married Dickie knowing exactly what sort of life I was in for, but when I tried to fit in I just couldn't. I just *couldn't* face living in Old Quinings from one year's end to another with no prospect of a change until I was buried in the family vault."

Kate smiled. She was not surprised.

" Why did I think I could ? " inquired Mrs. Morven, gazing out of the window in a thoughtful manner. " I must have been crazy, that's all."

" Or in love," suggested Kate.

" It's the same thing," said Mrs. Morven, nodding. " Yes, I fell for Dickie straight off. I was crazy about Dickie. I couldn't say no . . . and I went on liking him quite a lot. If Dickie had taken a firmer line it might have been different—it's just possible I might have settled down in time—but Dickie was not that kind. He was too soft, too nice, too civilised ; he let me go my own way." She laughed and added, " You know, Miss Hardy, I *still* like Dickie quite a lot, but not enough to go on living with him in the Manor House for ever and ever, amen."

Kate understood. She nodded. She decided that there was something very nice about this woman: she was so frank, so sincere, there was no nonsense about her. She spoke English without any trace of accent, it was only occasionally that an inflexion in her voice or the turn of a phrase betrayed the fact that she had spent so many years in America.

"But I didn't come here to bore you with that," continued Mrs. Morven. "That's past—it's no use crying over spilt milk. What I came about was . . . yes, here it is!" She took a crumpled envelope out of her bag and handed it to Kate.

"You want me to read it?" asked Kate, taking it.

"Please," said Mrs. Morven.

Kate unfolded a sheet of paper, which looked as if it had been torn from a child's exercise-book. The writing upon it was uneven and straggly:

Mister Morven has gave the Dower Hous to a lady friend and goes there every nite.

"But—that's—horrible!" cried Kate.

"I know," agreed Mrs. Morven. "It's quite disgusting, isn't it? At first I thought I wouldn't take any notice of it and then I changed my mind. I thought I would come and——"

Kate's face was burning. "Mrs. Morven, I can only say it isn't true," she declared. "You may not believe me, but——"

"Oh, I believe you," said Mrs. Morven, smiling. "As a matter of fact, I went to the lawyers yesterday and they told me the Dower House had been sold at a very high figure, so no doubt the rest of it is false, too."

"He comes to see me sometimes, of course," said Kate in a low voice. "He comes—perhaps twice a week. We're friends. We have a good deal in common——"

"You would. I mean you're clever, too," said Mrs. Morven naïvely. She sighed and added, "It's a pity, but it can't be helped."

Kate gazed at her.

"I'm disappointed," explained Mrs. Morven.

"You're disappointed?"

"Oh, I didn't expect anything very *lurid*, Dickie isn't that kind of person; but I thought there might be something in it—no smoke without fire, as they say."

"You want to divorce him?"

"Well, wouldn't that be the sensible thing? It seems silly to go on as we're doing, doesn't it, Miss Hardy? I wouldn't be sorry to be free—and Dickie wants an heir."

Kate was silent for a few moments and then she said, "What does Mr. Morven think about it?"

"I haven't seen him," Mrs. Morven replied. "I'm staying in town with some friends. I motored down. It's very difficult to know what to do for the best."

Kate felt unable to help her.

"Oh, well," said Mrs. Morven, rising, "I won't take up any more of your time. Don't say anything to Dickie, of course. My lawyer advised me not to see him until I had decided what I wanted to do . . . it would be fun to look in at the Manor, but I had better not. Good-bye, Miss Hardy."

"But please stay and have a cup of tea, or a glass of sherry or something," cried Kate.

"Well, that's very kind of you . . ." said Mrs. Morven, hesitating.

"Do stay. I'm just going to have tea," urged Kate.

Tea was ready in the morning-room so they went in and sat down. Now that the business part of their talk was over and the air cleared it was more comfortable, and Mrs. Morven, throwing off her coat, settled into an easy-chair. She was a madonna type, thought Kate, looking at her with pleasure . . . dark hair and eyes, perfect features and a matt-white complexion. Kate was not surprised that Richard Morven had fallen for her and credited her with all the graces. Any man would . . . and it was more than probable that many men had . . . not only Richard. Perhaps there was a man in the background, urging her to get a divorce. That might account for a good deal, thought Kate.

"I wonder who wrote that horrible letter," said Mrs. Morven thoughtfully, as she took a cup of tea from her hostess. "It might have been Mrs. Haygarth; she always hated me. I don't know if you've seen the Haygarths, Miss Hardy. They're very good servants, of course—Dickie has had them for years—but there's something rather sinister about them."

Kate said she had not seen them.

" Haygarth isn't so bad," declared Mrs. Morven. " He's thin and melancholy, but you know where you are with him. Mrs. Haygarth is pleasant on the surface—always smiling and plausible—but you can't trust her a yard. She's a *poisonous* woman," declared Mrs. Morven vehemently.

" But surely a woman like Mrs. Haygarth wouldn't be so illiterate," objected Kate.

" She might have pretended to be illiterate, mightn't she ? " suggested Mrs. Morven.

Kate disliked the subject. She changed it by asking after Susan.

" Susan ? " said Mrs. Morven with a puzzled frown.

" Your daughter," explained Kate, looking at her guest in surprise.

" Oh, yes, of course. It sounds funny to hear her called Susan."

" Isn't that her name ? "

" Not now," replied Mrs. Morven, accepting a scone. " You see she was always a very difficult child—I can't tell you how difficult she was—and a friend advised me to take her to a very clever doctor in New York. I had taken her to all sorts of doctors and psychiatrists but they had never done her any good. I was quite desperate about her, Miss Hardy. Dr. Schneider seemed to understand her at once. He diagnosed the trouble the very first time he saw her ; she was living in the wrong colours, Dr. Schneider said. He advised me to have her bedroom redecorated in shades of green—green is her colour, Miss Hardy—and he told me she must always wear green and eat plenty of salads and green vegetables. Her name was wrong, too (Susan is a pink name, Dr. Schneider says), so we changed it to Lilias."

" How—interesting ! " said Kate feebly. She could think of nothing else to say.

" You may think the whole thing rather crazy," said

Mrs. Morven with an apologetic air. "Quite a lot of people think it crazy. But really, Miss Hardy, I was so desperate about Lilias I would have tried anything—just anything—to get her right."

"I hope the treatment was successful?"

Mrs. Morven hesitated. "Well, I can't say I notice much change so far, but of course it's bound to take a long time to undo all the harm."

"I'm sorry she's so delicate."

"Not delicate, exactly. But she's very, very difficult to manage. Really, Miss Hardy, you wouldn't believe the trouble I've had with Lilias . . . and I'm afraid this trip to Europe will put her back a lot. I meant to leave her in the States with my sister so that Dr. Schneider could have her under observation but she wouldn't stay. I dare say that sounds funny to you but you don't know Lilias. If she can't have what she wants she gets sick at once—so I had to bring her along." Mrs. Morven sighed and added, "Now she's here I don't know what to do with her, whether to leave her in London with my friends or take her with me to Switzerland. I'm going to Switzerland next week for a little holiday."

"It does sound rather a problem."

"Yes, it is. I could take her with me, of course." She paused and smiled somewhat ruefully. "Oh, well, I guess Lilias will have to tag along, but it won't be so much fun for me."

Kate could well believe it. Mrs. Morven was a most attractive creature. To have a child—and a difficult child at that—tagging along wherever she went would cramp her style a good deal; but Kate was even more sorry for the child. Kate had always had a soft spot for Richard Morven's unwanted daughter. She said suddenly and impulsively and without due consideration, "I'll keep her for you, Mrs. Morven. Send her here."

Mrs. Morven was amazed, and not unnaturally, at this offer from a complete stranger, from a woman whom she had just accused of carrying on an illicit intrigue with her husband. She would not hear of such a thing, she declared. Lilias was difficult, she would be a bother. Miss Hardy had no idea what she was offering to undertake. It was very, very kind, but no, she would not *hear* of it. After some persuasion, however, Mrs. Morven began to weaken. She agreed that it would be extremely pleasant to spend a couple of weeks in Switzerland without her daughter hanging round her neck. It would be a complete holiday—which her doctor said she required. Eventually and with many protestations of gratitude she accepted the invitation—with the proviso that if Lilias didn't want to come it was all off, because it was no use trying to make Lilias do anything she didn't want.

The next half-hour was occupied by Mrs. Morven's account of her child's idiosyncracies (which were many, and of an alarming nature) and by a long list of foods : some of which Lilias must eat, others which she must not be allowed to touch. The list was formidable, and before Mrs. Morven was half-way through Kate was completely muddled by the *régime* laid down by Dr. Schneider for the benefit of her prospective guest. The foods in the " must " category would not be easy to procure in post-war England, but she would have to consult Martha and do her best. When Kate went to the door and saw her visitor drive away in the Daimler belonging to her London friends, she was already regretting her hospitable impulse and hoping with all her heart that Lilias wouldn't want to come.

Part Two

CHAPTER ELEVEN

IT HAD BEEN raining all day, the best kind of day for writing, and the new story about Stephen Slade had progressed considerably. At tea-time Kate went into her bedroom to brush her hair, and discovered a man in brown drill overalls working at the window. He had taken out the sash and was fitting new cords.

" Thank goodness you've come at last, Mr. Seager ! " exclaimed Kate.

He turned and looked at her and she saw that it was not Mr. Seager ; it was Walter Stack.

" Practically all the windows need new cords," said Walter gravely. " It will cost a good deal but it will have to be done sooner or later."

Kate was taken aback and disconcerted, the more so because she had a feeling that beneath his matter-of-fact manner there was embarrassment.

" I wish you wouldn't ! " she exclaimed impulsively.

He did not pretend to misunderstand. " Why shouldn't I ? " he demanded. " It's a useful job and I like it."

" It's all right if you like it," admitted Kate.

" The point is, do you want all the windows done or not ? "

" Yes, please," said Kate meekly. She stood and watched him for a few minutes and saw that he worked quickly and competently. " Wouldn't it be easier somewhere else ? " asked Kate at last.

He did not reply.

Kate hesitated. The first night, when he had come to supper, he had looked confident and happy. Now he looked —different. There was defiance in his attitude. She suspected bitterness. "Will you come and have tea with me, Major Stack?" said Kate.

"Just Stack, please," said Walter without looking up. "It's more suitable, you'll agree. The war was an interlude. This was my job before the war. I'm back in my proper place."

"And you've put me in mine," added Kate ruefully.

"I didn't mean that," said Walter quickly. "You're very kind. I don't want to be ungracious, but it's better to have things straight."

"Is there any reason why you shouldn't come and have tea with me?"

"The best of reasons," he replied, looking up and smiling. "I don't knock off work till five."

"Come at five, then," said Kate, and she went away.

She was doubtful if he would come. She was quite absurdly anxious that he should come. She found herself glancing at the clock and listening for sounds of movement upstairs. At five minutes past five the door opened and Walter came in. He had taken off his overalls and was wearing grey flannel trousers and a brown pullover with a polo collar.

"Come along," said Kate, smiling at him. "I've been waiting for you."

He sat down and accepted a cup of tea. "It's very kind," he said gravely. "But you're making it difficult, Miss Hardy. You're putting me in such a difficult position."

"That's nonsense," said Kate, smiling at him. "I defy you to produce any sensible reason why you shouldn't come and have tea with me when you've finished work."

He was silent.

"You can't," declared Kate triumphantly.

"Not really, but——"

"Walter, listen to me," said Kate. (She had decided on this mode of address after due deliberation, for obviously it was impossible for her to address her guest as "Stack.") "Just listen to me," said Kate. "It's because you're in an invidious position that you see difficulties where there are none. When your work is over for the day you are free. You are yourself. If I ask you to tea you come as my friend —at least I hope so."

" I need friends badly," admitted Walter. " I don't seem to have many in Old Quinings."

" So that's the trouble," said Kate in a thoughtful voice.

Walter helped himself to a little gingerbread cake. " That's the trouble," he said. " I shall live it down in time, of course, but at present it isn't easy. My old friends don't like me very much. They dislike the way I speak, for one thing." He paused. " You know, Miss Hardy," he continued in a thoughtful voice, " I believe that's the real cause of the trouble—such a silly little detail, isn't it ? "

Kate was not sure. It seemed a silly little detail, but was it ? She had a feeling that it was a symbol of everything Walter had become, a symbol of the fact that Walter, who had been one of them, was one of them no longer.

" It's natural for me to speak as I do," continued Walter. " I could go back to the old way but it wouldn't be natural —so why should I ? "

" You couldn't," declared Kate. " It would make things worse."

" The odd thing is," he continued, " the strangest thing of all is that the man who used to be my best friend is the very one who is now the most difficult to get on with. Reuben Doubleday and I used to do everything together ; we used to go off for long days on the moor, fishing or rabbiting. Sometimes we fought, but only in a friendly way. All boys have their quarrels."

" You've changed, of course."

" So has Reuben," said Walter sadly. " He isn't the fellow he used to be. He's drinking a bit—and that's no good to any one. During the war Reuben was Mr. Seager's head workman and now that I've come back he's got to take second place. He doesn't like that."

" He wouldn't," nodded Kate.

" But it's perfectly fair ! " cried Walter. " Mr. Seager

is obliged by law to take me back in my old place. If Reuben was getting less pay I could understand it, but he's getting exactly the same. Why should he resent it? Why should every one resent it?"

"Every one?"

"Practically every one. I'm not very popular in Old Quinings."

Kate was silent for a few moments and then she said, "There are other places—there are other things you can do. I could help you to find a job, Walter. I know Sir Adam Bancroft, the director of the aircraft factory at Northport. He's always on the outlook for men like you. You would have more scope in a job like that, more chance to get on. It's absurd for you to come back here to Old Quinings and think you can wash out the last six years."

"This is my place," said Walter. "It's very kind of you, but this is my place."

"It isn't!" she cried. "It doesn't fit you. Why try to cram yourself into a round hole?"

"I'm glad you think I'm square," said Walter with a wry smile.

"Tell me why," said Kate imperiously.

"All right, I will," he said, handing in his cup for more tea. "There are two main reasons why I intend to stay in Old Quinings. First of all this is my own job, and I'm determined to keep it. Neither Reuben nor any one else shall drive me out of my job. And secondly, there's my mother," said Walter, his face softening. "I promised my mother I would come back and live with her and I intend to keep my promise. I want to live with her. I want to make her life easy and happy and comfortable. Mother has had a pretty hard time of it one way and another. She's the best mother in the world. I owe everything to mother and it's time I did something for her. Does that satisfy you, Miss Hardy?"

"It ought to satisfy me," replied Kate in a low voice.

They were silent for a few minutes and then they began to talk about other things. Walter became cheerful and natural. He was interesting to Kate because he had his own ideas about things ; he had thought out social problems and had found answers to many of the questions which were puzzling people and unsettling their lives. Walter's answers were unusual and debatable but none the less interesting for that. Personality was the master-key to the problems of to-day—so Walter thought—he had found it so in his army career. Some people were born leaders ; why not use them in peace as in war ?

"Fascism ! " declared Kate.

"Fascism ! " echoed Walter in disgust. "The word is an absolute bogey. People cry ' fascism ' in horror-stricken tones and that damns everything. There are *horrible* things in the fascist system, we all know that, but don't let's damn a good thing because it happens to be in the system. Leadership is a good thing. It doesn't only mean leading men in battle, it means looking after them all the time. It means taking an interest in them, seeing that they keep fit and happy, solving their problems for them. That's leadership."

"Then your idea is that there should be groups of people under leaders——"

"You needn't call them leaders," interrupted Walter. "I know that sounds a bit too fascistic. My idea is that there should be groups in every town, in every village, with a man at the head who would look after their welfare and help them, if they needed help. People need looking after ; they *like* it if it's done in the right way. I know that from experience ; it isn't just theory."

"But, Walter——"

"Great Scot, look at the time ! " cried Walter, leaping to his feet. "I shall be late for supper—that's a certainty."

Kate pursued him to the door. "Come back soon. I haven't had a chance to tear your ideas to pieces ! " cried Kate, laughing.

He waved and ran for his life down the drive.

When he had gone, Kate returned to the morning-room and sat down at her desk, but instead of writing she leant her elbow on the desk, and, chin in hand, stared out of the window. A square peg in a round hole, thought Kate, and the pity of it was there were so many square holes waiting for a man like Walter. She had told Walter that she ought to be satisfied with his reasons for remaining in Old Quinings. She was not sure now whether this was true. She saw his point of view, of course. He was not going to be driven from the job which was his by right ; and she liked him all the better for that streak of stubbornness in his nature. She sympathised even more profoundly with his determination to do something for his mother. But what a· pity it was ! Walter's sacrifice would benefit nobody, not even Mrs. Stack. For Walter was unhappy (already he had lost his air of confidence and had become slightly embittered by the enmity he had incurred), and an unhappy Walter meant an unhappy Mrs. Stack. Walter had said he would live it down, but would he be able to ? In some ways Kate hoped not. He was wasted here. There was no future in his present job. She had mentioned Sir Adam Bancroft ; Sir Adam would take Walter like a shot. Walter was exactly the sort of man who would appeal to Sir Adam with his ideas about leadership, his experience of managing men and his distinguished war record. But it was not the slightest use writing to Sir Adam as long as Walter was determined to remain here, and Walter seemed immovable. With that chin of his—that firmly chiselled jaw—it was doubtful whether anything less dynamic than an atom bomb would move Walter out of Old Quinings.

CHAPTER TWELVE

NOTHING in the way of repairs had been done to the Dower House for years, so when Walter had finished putting new cords on the windows he started to mend door handles, to rehang doors that had sagged on their hinges, and to replace some of the worn boards in the floors. Wood was the real difficulty, but Walter possessed initiative and resource. He discovered an old partition in the attic which was serving no useful purpose, and he suggested that he should use this excellent wood not only for the floorboards but also for shelves. Kate was delighted that he should : Martha needed an extra shelf in the pantry, Kate wanted a shelf in her bedroom to hold books. In addition to this she discussed with Walter the feasibility of having shelves in the attic upon which she could store apples and pears from her orchard—when apples and pears appeared. Walter agreed that it would be an excellent plan, but added that it might have to wait ; there was no hurry about it anyhow. It surprised Kate considerably that she was allowed to have so many small jobs done ; for in London—and in most other places—only essential repairs were permitted ; workmen were busy mending bomb-damaged houses and erecting new ones. Mr. Seager explained the matter by saying things were different here. There was no bomb damage— the only bomb had fallen in the village duck-pond—and the erection of new houses had been given to a Wandlebury contractor, who, incidentally, was taking his time about it. Mr. Seager had now got all his men demobilised ; he was obliged to take them back whether he wanted to or not, so Miss Hardy could have anything she wanted done in reason.

"In reason, of course," repeated Mr. Seager, nodding solemnly. "In reason you can, provided it doesn't take wood."

It seemed quite mad to Kate, but nowadays so many

things seemed mad that one was getting—or had got—quite used to it.

" Couldn't your men build houses, Mr. Seager ? " she inquired. " Houses are wanted so badly."

" Why, of course they could," replied Mr. Seager in surprise. " Not *build* houses ! Of course they're not bricklayers, Miss Hardy, but they could put up these prefabs in half no time—they would, too, if I'd got the job. But it's a Government job, you see. The people will have to wait for their houses until the big contractor can spare the time for it."

" I see," said Kate, nodding.

" That's the way of it," said Mr. Seager, glad that he had been able to explain it so satisfactorily.

" Mr. Seager, are you satisfied with the arrangement ? " asked Kate.

" Well, there now, that's a question if you like ! I *ought* to be satisfied, Miss Hardy. It suits me from a business point of view. There's enough private work in Old Quinings to keep me going—there's work at the Manor alone that'll keep my men busy for weeks. Private work pays better, and I keep my old customers . . . but am I satisfied ? Not really. It gets my goat when I think of those prefabs. No, I'd rather put my men on the essential work—never mind the business point of view. That's the sort of fool I am."

Kate was getting to know Old Quinings now. She had been prevailed upon by Mrs. Barton to distribute the Parish Magazine, and this job took her to most of the houses and cottages and farms in the parish. It also took her away from her work, but that was a good thing in some ways, for a little outdoor exercise was beneficial. Besides, Kate had not come to Old Quinings with the intention of shutting herself away from her fellow human beings, she wanted to meet her new neighbours and understand them.

She met them. Sometimes she understood them but more often she did not.

Old Quinings was not as Kate had imagined it. She

had imagined an English village as a sort of Eden—with an occasional snake, of course. She had read Gray's *Elegy*, so she had thought of the people like that : ploughmen plodding home at night to their cosy homes where swallows twittered in the eaves and rosy-cheeked children waited to climb upon their knees. She had heard songs about the simple jovial life of the country—Widdicombe Fair, for instance ; she had read some of the modern exponents of village life, so she was prepared to find nature in the raw and a bucolic brand of socialism ; and, having thoroughly digested *Adam Bede*, she had realised that country people were not invariably chaste. But none of her reading prepared her for the extraordinary mixture of beauty and ugliness which went to the making of Old Quinings.

Richard Morven had told her there were queer things in Old Quinings—and how right he was ! The more she saw of the place the stranger and more incomprehensible it seemed. This strangeness and queerness might have been very valuable material to some authors, to authors who went in for that sort of thing, but it was no use to Kate ; her books were born and nurtured in a different atmosphere altogether. Kate toyed with the idea of a " little book " about Old Quinings (her publishers would be pleased, she knew, for her name would be sufficient to sell it, and " little books " were fashionable at the moment), a " little book " illustrated with woodcuts which would reveal the inner soul of an English village to people who were so unfortunate as to live in towns. But it was only an idea, and in her heart of hearts she knew it would come to nothing, for the truth was Kate did not understand Old Quinings and she had a feeling she never would. Perhaps if you had been born and bred in this place—or in a place of this kind— you might understand its curious mentality, or perhaps not. Kate did not know.

Old Quinings was like a human being with a complex personality : intricate, moody, gay and sullen, good and evil. You thought you had found a clue to Old Quinings and then you found you had lost it. You were always being surprised by the goodness and badness of people, by their stupidity and common sense. People were like this in towns (everybody was like this to a certain extent), but it did not show so much because people who lived in towns were more sophisticated and took care to conform to a pattern ; they were afraid of being thought different from their neighbours. The people here did not mind being thought different. They behaved like themselves, not as they thought other people expected them to behave. Like icebergs floating in the sea, there was more below the surface than above, more invisible than visible ; and not only more bulk, but bulk more important, more dangerous to the mariner. Sometimes the berg lost its balance and turned over—you could look out for trouble when that happened.

If Kate had been less interested in human nature she might have been content to live here and take her neighbours as she found them without bothering to understand, but she was intensely interested in human nature (what could be more interesting ?) and puzzles intrigued her—besides, she liked to have things tidy. Her own mind was clear-cut, reasonable and logical. She wanted to straighten out the tangles of Old Quinings to her own satisfaction.

Cleanliness was next to godliness, so Kate believed. She had valued cleanliness highly until she began to distribute Parish Magazines for Mrs. Barton, but now she began to think other things mattered more. Mrs. Robinson's cottage was as clean as a whistle. Everything was polished, her children were well dressed and well fed—and utterly miserable. There was cleanliness in the Robinson cottage but no comfort, or at least no comfort for the heart. Mrs. Fraught's cottage had a curious smell—it smelt of dirty dish-cloths—greasy pans cluttered the sink and the hearth-rug needed mending, but the fire was bright, there was a nice fat tabby sitting in front of it, the children had merry faces and ragged clothes. Mrs. Curtis had a comfortable cottage, clean and tidy. There was a child sitting by the fire with a flushed swollen face and tired eyes. " Toothache,

that's all," said Mrs. Curtis briskly. "Jimmy makes a lot
of fuss about nothing. It ain't worth getting the doctor for
toothache, I can treat 'im for that myself," and nothing
Kate could do or say would persuade the apparently sane
woman that the child was ill, that the doctor should be
summoned, and, if it were toothache, the tooth should come
out. Mrs. Curtis preferred her own remedies, which were
utterly disgusting and calculated to induce septicæmia.
Kate came out of the cottage boiling with rage ; what could
you do with a woman like that ? You were helpless—quite
helpless.

Then there was Abijah—a revolting person—but how
hard he worked ! Sometimes he was still hard at work in
Kate's garden at nine o'clock at night, sometimes Kate
went out and told him to go home. She had expected him
to ask for overtime pay, but it had never occurred to him
to ask for it, and he was surprised beyond measure when
he received what was obviously his due.

Selina Morven had not appeared to Kate ; and Kate
was glad of this, but all the same she was interested in her
ghost. She mentioned it to one or two people in the village
but the subject seemed unpopular. Either Old Quinings
was not interested in Selina, or else—or else too interested,
thought Kate, trying to fathom the inner significance of
the apparent indifference.

Miss Morris was a different kind of puzzle. Her cottage
was tiny, she lived in it by herself—a little elderly woman
with a worn face. Kate knew nothing about Miss Morris
except her name, but saw at once that Miss Morris was a
well-educated woman.

"The Parish Magazine ! " said Miss Morris when she
opened the door. "Oh, yes—thank you very much—and
I always give Mrs. Barton a small contribution towards the
home for Unmarried Mothers." The small contribution
was half a crown, taken from a shabby purse in which
the remainder of the money was coppers. She was extremely
poor, she was under-nourished, she had seen better days,
she was interested in Unmarried Mothers to the extent of

denying herself the necessities of life on their behalf. Who and what was Miss Morris ?

Mrs. Underwood's cottage was Kate's next port of call. Mrs. Underwood was distinguished by a large question mark in Mrs. Barton's list, but it had not been explained to Kate what the question mark signified, and her sense of duty impelled her to knock at Mrs. Underwood's door. There was a good deal of scuffling before the door was opened and the owner of the cottage appeared, and Kate had time to wonder afresh what the question mark implied. Mrs. Underwood was a fresh-looking person of uncertain age ; she was clean and smiling. Her cottage was clean too. She insisted that Miss Hardy should come in for a cup of tea, and Miss Hardy, who was feeling a trifle jaded, accepted the invitation. She was sorry afterwards, not because there was anything the matter with the tea (it was excellent tea and the china was above reproach), but because Mrs. Underwood herself was poisonous. Kate found it a curious experience—almost a terrifying experience—to sit and drink Mrs. Underwood's tea and listen to her conversation, listen to her discussing the affairs of her neighbours—pulling them to pieces, vilifying them, dragging their skeletons out of their cupboards—and smiling sweetly all the time. It would not have been nearly so horrible if Mrs. Underwood had looked like a ghoul, if she had been ugly and misshapen in body and not only in soul. The poison would not have affected Kate so potently if it had not been disguised in cream.

When Kate came out of Mrs. Underwood's cottage she drew a deep breath of fresh air, but it was some time before she managed to get rid of the poisonous miasma. She found herself looking askance at the cheerful rubicond countenance of the butcher as he measured out her sausages, and at the friendly smiles of the girl in the post office when she went in to buy stamps. Kate was reminded of a story by Algernon Blackwood about a man who discovered that beneath the simple rational life of the town he loved there were evil things, things which could not be spoken of and which were never revealed to the light of day. Was Old Quinings like that town? No, said Kate firmly to herself. Mrs. Underwood is like that town, but Mrs. Underwood is not Old Quinings.

These were just a few examples of the things Kate discovered as she went about the village distributing the Parish Magazine.

Kate saw quite a lot of Miss Crease, for Miss Crease lived next door to the Dower House, and it was difficult if not impossible for Kate to slink out of her gate without being spotted by her neighbour and detained for conversation. Miss Crease was so ugly as to be sinister, her face was dark-skinned and crooked, her neck was set forward on her high shoulders, and her skimpy white hair was drawn back from her forehead and twisted into a " bun." (The first time she had seen Miss Crease, Kate had been obliged to hide a smile, not at the poor woman's appearance, which was a disaster, but at a thought which her appearance invoked. If Milly had been there she would have nudged Kate and whispered, " Just the sort of person to put in your next book." But she wasn't, of course. You didn't put people like that in books. Kate never put real live people into her books ; there was no necessity.) Despite her unfortunate appearance there were good qualities in Miss Crease. She was courageous, she bore her infirmities without grumbling, and she possessed a certain dry humour which appealed to Kate.

Miss Crease was always full of the latest news and liked to retail it. She obtained her news in various and devious ways. Annie was a help, of course. Annie had relations in Old Quinings and picked up juicy bits of gossip as a blackbird picks up worms, and—to pursue the metaphor—having picked up the worm she would fly home with it wriggling in her beak and feed it in tasty morsels to her nestling. But Miss Crease was not entirely dependent upon Annie ; she had her own methods of worming bits of information out of her neighbours. She lay in wait for her victims and summoned them imperiously, ignoring their reluctance to obey. Sometimes she obtained her information by asking straight out and at other times approached the subject obliquely ; occasionally she pounced and startled her victim into admitting some fact he had hoped to hide, following her pounce with a spot of third degree . . . but her favourite method and by far her most successful was to make an erroneous statement—a fantastic statement—with an air of assurance and wait for her victim to correct it.

Quite early in their acquaintance Kate discovered Miss Crease's little game, and far from discouraging it, played up to her in a lively manner. Kate rather enjoyed playing ball. She told Miss Crease all sorts of things that didn't matter, but nothing she didn't want to tell. Kate was too quick-witted to be caught by pouncing, she was too clear headed to be bamboozled by third degree, and when Miss Crease employed her favourite procedure, and made some wild statement which was palpably untrue, Kate merely raised her eyebrows and exclaimed, " Oh, Miss Crease, you don't say so ! "

In spite of this, Miss Crease liked her new neighbour quite a lot. Perhaps it was because she was a little tired of brow-beating people and was gratified to find someone who could not be brow-beaten.

" Miss Hardy ! " cried Miss Crease, waving and beckoning to Kate, who was off for her morning walk with the last four copies of the Parish Magazine tucked under her arm. " Miss Hardy, come here. You aren't in a hurry, are you ? "

" I am, rather," said Kate, holding up the magazines for her to see.

" You don't suppose anybody reads those things, do you ? I use them for lighting the fire."

" And they're excellent for wrapping fish—such nice thick paper," nodded Kate.

Miss Crease had reached the gate by this time. She leant her elbows on it and said, " Richard's wife has gone off with a third-class actor. He's going to divorce her."

" Not really ? " said Kate, raising her eyebrows in surprise.

They eyed one another warily.

"Wanda is a pretty creature," said Miss Crease. "It's a pity she has such a bad complexion, isn't it?"

"Do you know," said Kate very thoughtfully, "do you know, I don't think I ever saw a pretty woman with a bad complexion. It seems impossible to me."

Miss Crease hesitated. Should she pounce or not? The rumour was very vague. Annie had heard from the butcher's boy, who had heard from someone else that someone had seen a big car drive in at the Dower House gates and the lady in it had looked like Mrs. Morven. Unfortunately Miss Crease was obliged to rest in the afternoon so she had not seen the car herself, and Annie had been making jam. Miss Crease sighed and decided that it was too vague—and too unlikely. She changed the subject.

"Stack is home, I hear. He's a general or something, isn't he?"

"A major," said Kate, smiling. "And he hasn't got the V.C.—merely a D.S.O."

"Seager will be glad to have him back if he hasn't got too big for his boots," declared Miss Crease. "It's a pity when people get too big for their boots. Don't you agree, Miss Hardy?"

"They can always get new boots," suggested Kate with a thoughtful air.

"So he's going away, is he? Getting a better job, I suppose?"

"I don't know," said Kate truthfully.

"I thought you said he was."

"No; I inferred that he *could* find another job if this one pinched him."

So far Kate had done quite well, but she was beginning to get a trifle hot and she was aware that unless she kept perfectly cool she might say more than she intended. It was time to go, and Kate went. She had the advantage there, her line of retreat was open, for Miss Crease was lame and could not pursue her down the road.

CHAPTER THIRTEEN

By SATURDAY morning all the Parish Magazines had been
delivered ; this was lucky, because Milly and Minta arrived
in the afternoon. They had accepted Kate's invitation to
come for Minta's birthday and spend the week-end . . .
they wanted to see what sort of a house Kate had bought ;
it was natural curiosity.

There was only one taxi in Old Quinings ; Kate engaged
it and went to the station herself and walked up and down
the platform, waiting for the train to arrive. She felt a
little nervous, which was ridiculous when you came to
think of it, because it didn't matter a hoot whether Milly
and Minta liked the house or not . . . but perhaps it was
not *that* so much, thought Kate, trying to analyse the cause
of her uneasiness ; perhaps she was nervous because the
advent of Milly and Minta would disturb her peace. It
had been so peaceful here. Already Kate felt settled in a
comfortable rut. Already she felt a member of the little
community . . . it was as if she had lived in Old Quinings
for years.

Milly and Minta were in their best clothes (how strange
London clothes looked in the country, thought Kate as she
ran down the platform to meet her guests), they were also
on their best behaviour ; but having parted on strained
terms (to say the least of it) things were just a little difficult,
and after the first fervour of greeting there were embar-
rassing moments of silence broken by sudden spurts of
conversation. Fortunately it was Minta's birthday, so, once
they were in the taxi, Kate presented her with a cheque
(Martha was to give her the pullover), and Minta, who had
been hoping for a cheque and wondering how large it was
likely to be, was fairly well satisfied with her aunt's
generosity.

Milly was surprised at the size of Kate's property, she

had not expected anything so imposing, it was definitely a
" place." In one way Milly was pleased, because she could
imagine herself saying to her friends, " I spent the week-end
at my sister's place in the country, near Wandlebury, you
know, etc., etc.", but in another way she was not pleased,
for how *unfair* it was that Kate should possess such a large
and attractive abode and she herself merely a smallish flat
in London ! Not that Milly would have exchanged with
Kate, of course—good gracious no !—Milly wouldn't have
lived in a dull little hole like Old Quinings for worlds.

Kate's guests started to exclaim with admiration before
they were inside the house. It was obvious that this was
their " line." Kate felt pretty certain that they had discussed things thoroughly before they came—they were fond
of discussing things thoroughly—and decided to admire
everything they saw and to be as pleasant as possible to
their hostess. Kate's sudden defection had given them a
shock, its effects were delayed but none the less potent, and
on thinking it over they realised the foolishness of quarrelling
irrevocably with Kate, who, if not their bread and butter,
was in the same metaphor their roof.

" How lovely ! " they cried with one voice as the taxi
drove up to the door.

" What a pretty entrance ! " exclaimed Minta.

" What a beautiful hall ! " cried Milly.

Their bedrooms charmed them ; the view of the garden
which could be seen from the windows was delightful ; they
waxed positively lyrical over the bathrooms.

Now that she saw it again, Milly remembered the
furniture quite well, and remembered where each piece
had stood in her parents' house. Her sentimental reminis-
cences were a little trying to her hostess.

" This was Father's chair," said Milly in a hushed
voice. " I remember Father *sitting* in it—on the right of
the fireplace in the drawing-room. Oh, dear, isn't it *sad*,"
said Milly almost tearfully.

" I can't see anything *sad* about it," objected her
daughter. " It isn't even a very comfortable chair."

"You're too young to remember Grandfather, dear," returned Milly. "And as for not being a very *comfortable* chair, I can't see what that has got to do with it."

"I expect Minta means he is more comfortable in heaven," said Kate briskly.

Minta giggled—she found her aunt amusing—but Milly was scandalised.

"I can remember Father *sitting* in that chair, so of *course* I feel sad," said Milly in reproachful tones.

Minta took up the challenge. "Well, I must say if you only remember him when you see a mouldy old chair——" began Minta, and then suddenly was silent.

This little exchange cured Milly of her sentimental reactions to the furniture, or at least prevented her from expressing them aloud. She still felt aggrieved that Kate should have the furniture—every bit of it—and was convinced, in spite of Mr. Chester's assurances to the contrary, that somehow or other she had been done out of her rights. She did not want the furniture, of course, for the flat was furnished already (and this was large old-fashioned stuff, quite unsuitable for town), but Milly had the type of brain which could retain two totally different and conflicting ideas at the same moment, and she could argue about them for hours without allowing them to meet or to affect each other in the least.

By dinner-time Milly felt quite exhausted by the emotions raised in her bosom and by her efforts to disguise them from her sister's eyes. A glass of sherry revived her considerably, however . . . and the dinner was excellent, consisting of onion soup, roast chicken and vegetables from the Dower House garden, chocolate pudding and apples. Mr. Morven had sent the apples from the Manor House store-room. He had told Kate that they were hagloe crabs.

Milly enjoyed her dinner, but here again her enjoyment was tempered by the feeling that it wasn't fair. You couldn't get things like this in town, so why should Kate have them? She was extremely irritated when her daughter remarked that it was the best meal she had eaten for years.

"I do my best," said Milly, trying to make the words sound like a joke, but not succeeding very well.

"Your best isn't very good," replied Minta. "Oh, I'm not complaining ; I can always go out and get a meal somewhere when my tummy begins to flap against my ribs."

"Minta !" exclaimed her mother. "What a vulgar way to talk !"

"Yes, isn't it," nodded Minta. "But hunger is a vulgar emotion—and when I say emotion I mean emotion," she added firmly.

"I'm often hungry too," complained Milly. "You never think of *me*. I don't go out and gorge myself at restaurants, I cook and scrub and stand in queues for hours on end. It's most exhausting and I'm sure I've lost pounds in the last few weeks."

"Perhaps, but I must say you don't look it," retorted her daughter callously.

Kate did not agree with Minta ; she thought Milly had lost quite a lot of weight and looked tired and worn into the bargain. She persuaded Milly to go to bed early and accompanied her to her room to see she had all she required. When Kate came down she found Minta in the garden admiring the roses, which were just beginning to bloom.

"You've got a gardener," said Minta, pointing to evidences of his work.

"Yes," agreed Kate. "Yes, I had some difficulty in getting one, and the one I've got is rather a horrible creature. I never meant to engage him."

"What *do* you mean ?" asked Minta in surprise.

"I mean," said Kate, laughing somewhat ruefully, "I mean I didn't really engage him at all, he just came and started work. He works well, I must say, and he seems to know all about it . . . but I don't like him."

"Why don't you tell him to go ?" Minta, not unnaturally, inquired.

"I did," replied Kate. "I summoned up my courage and told him to go away, but he was back here, working,

the next morning. Oh, I know it sounds silly but I can't
help it—and of course I do need a gardener very badly."

" You could refuse to pay him, Aunt Kate."

" No," said Kate firmly. The idea had occurred to her,
of course, but she could not entertain it for a moment. If
Abijah insisted upon working in her garden he must be paid.

They walked round the vegetable garden where Abijah
had spent most of his working hours, and spent them to
good purpose. The peas were coming on well—they had
been put in as plants—there were beans and lettuces and a
host of other vegetables. Everything looked in a flourishing
condition and Minta commented on the fact.

" I think you're very lucky indeed to have him," said
Minta firmly. " I don't know what on earth you're
complaining about."

" It's just that I don't like him," said Kate feebly.

" Are you happy here, Aunt Kate ? "

" What do you think ? "

" I'm afraid you are," said Minta with a sigh. " You
look—you look *contented*. Of course I see the charm of it,
you know. In fact, I think the country is definitely the best
place to live—for older people like you."

" Thank you," said her aunt, smiling.

" We miss you," continued Minta. " Both of us do in
different ways . . . and not only because we were more
comfortable when you and Martha were there. I thought
perhaps you might get tired of it and come back——"

" No," said Kate, and then—as plain speaking seemed
to be the order of the day—she added, " I like peace ; not
only country peace but also the domestic variety."

" Oh, Aunt Kate, I don't know what you mean ! "

" You know exactly what I mean, Minta," smiled
Kate.

" But we don't quarrel, mother and I. We only squabble
—it's quite different."

" Equally unpleasant to my mind," said Kate, closing
the conversation.

CHAPTER FOURTEEN

SUNDAY was fine and warm, which was all the more fortunate because Kate and her guests had been invited to
tea at the Manor. Kate had not been there before, which
seemed a little odd, but Richard Morven was old-fashioned
and would not ask Miss Hardy to his house unchaperoned.
The walk through the woods was very pleasant, for it was
shady and cool and the sunshine fell through the fresh green
leaves dappling the path with light and shade. Here and
there the trees had been thinned and there were vistas of
parkland with cattle grazing.

" Does all this belong to Mr. Morven ? " asked Milly in
amazement.

" All this and a good deal more," replied Kate. " The
moor belongs to him and the village ; he has a splendid
orchard and a home farm which supplies the whole neighbourhood with milk. Those are his cows, of course—lovely
fat cows, aren't they ? "

" How old is he ? " asked Milly, who was not interested
in cows.

" About forty-five, I should think," said Kate, smiling.

The Manor House burst upon their view quite suddenly
as they emerged from the woods. They saw it across the
broad space of a smooth green lawn flanked by a herbaceous
border. It was a beautiful example of its period : a typical
Queen Anne mansion, not very large, as large houses go,
but dignified and serene. They stood for a few moments
looking at it in silence and then they saw their host hurrying
to meet them across the grass. Kate had not seen Richard
Morven for several days—not since Wanda's visit—and she
felt slightly embarrassed. She was glad that the others
were there.

All the usual things were said as they walked towards
the house. Milly and Minta chattered politely and Mr.

Morven listened and answered and smiled. Kate stole several glances at her host, wondering if he knew his wife was in London, but it was impossible to guess from his face and manner whether he knew or not. She herself had heard no more from Wanda Morven and was completely in the dark as to her intentions.

Tea was laid in the library, which was a long-shaped room with books on three sides from floor to ceiling, the fourth side consisting of three windows with pictures upon the wall space between. The chairs were of dark-green leather, slightly shabby but deep and comfortable. There was a large gate-legged table covered with papers and writing materials, and another table, exactly similar, bore teacups and plates of bread and butter and a goodly array of cakes. The books fascinated Kate and drew her eyes like a magnet : what a magnificent reference library, and how useful it would be to her in her work ! She wondered if she could ask Mr. Morven for permission to browse here occasionally. It was a natural request and yet she felt a little shy of making it.

The tea-tray was brought in by a bustling woman with a smiling face. She seemed particularly interested in Kate —or so Kate imagined—staring at her with unconcealed interest as she arranged the tea-things on the table and rearranged the plates. She seemed to be taking an unnecessarily long time over the work, and Mr. Morven evidently thought so too.

"That will do, thank you," he said. "We can manage now, Mrs. Haygarth."

She went reluctantly, shutting the door behind her very softly, and Kate was conscious of a feeling of relief. Wanda Morven was right, thought Kate. The woman was unpleasant ; she might have written the anonymous message (Kate did not think she would hesitate to make mischief if she thought it would be to her advantage), but what advantage did she expect t' gain from upsetting Mrs. Morven ? It seemed to Kate that Mrs. Haygarth had an extremely comfortable post and her interest lay in keeping it, whereas the person who had written the anonymous message had written it to stir up trouble and disturb the peace.

There was a fifth place laid at the table and as they sat down, Richard explained that he was expecting Miss Carlyle.

" I think you'll like her, Miss Hardy," he said. " She teaches at the village school. She's doing an excellent job. There's a boy called Tommy Rogers ; he's thirteen now and brilliantly clever ; Miss Carlyle and I have been putting our heads together over young Tommy. He must be given his chance."

" I've met Miss Carlyle——" began Kate, but at that moment the door opened and the fourth guest was announced.

Miss Carlyle apologised for being late but did not explain what had delayed her. She looked upset, Kate thought, but perhaps that was because she had hurried. Mr. Morven made the introductions and they all settled down. Milly, as chief guest, was seated upon her host's right, and Kate was amused to see that she was taking a good deal of trouble to impress him. She had a habit of turning her head slowly and looking up at the person she was talking to in an appealing way, and opening her large brown eyes very wide indeed. Kate sometimes thought Milly must have practised this in front of a mirror, but she was aware the suspicion was unworthy. It might be perfectly natural for Milly to behave like that to people she didn't know well. Milly was always at her best with strangers and her best was very good. It was unfortunate that she should show such a much less attractive facet of her personality to people who knew her well. If she could be so charming to outsiders, why not to her relations ? It seemed unfair. It was all the more unfair, thought Kate, because it was so difficult for her relations to agree enthusiastically with the enthusiastic enconiums of those who, meeting Milly for the first time, were delighted by her charm. Kate hated insincerity, yet, in a case like this, insincerity was forced upon her ; either insincerity or the certainty of earning the reputation for jealousy. But it was not Milly's fault—not really—for Milly did not understand. Milly did not realise how much happier she would be if she thought more of other people's feelings and less of her own. She could not see that all her troubles arose from her own selfishness, her own stupidity, her own lack of consideration. She was like the people who have eyes but see not, and ears but hear not. One had to make allowances for people who were blind and deaf . . . usually Kate could.

The conversation was general. Miss Carlyle spoke of her star pupil, Tommy Rogers, and told Mr. Morven with some pride that she had managed to persuade his parents to allow him to continue his education instead of taking him away from school at Christmas so that he could become an errand boy and earn his keep. Milly and Minta described a play they had seen in London. Milly said London was terribly crowded these days and it was terribly difficult to get food. She sighed and said she envied those whose lot was cast in pleasant country places . . . at this moment Kate happened to catch Minta's eye and received an exceedingly vulgar wink.

After tea they went out, and their host walked them round the garden. Five is an awkward number, of course, so the party fell quite naturally into two groups : Mr. Morven leading the way with Milly and Minta, the others following at their leisure. Kate had expected to find Miss Carlyle interesting to talk to. She found her very interesting indeed, for she was quite willing to talk about her work as long as Kate would listen. She told some amusing stories about her children, copying their accents to the life.

" You don't find the work dull," said Kate. " I mean, I can see you don't ; you couldn't talk about it in such an interesting way if you did."

" I couldn't do it at all if I found it dull. It would be impossible."

" Yes, I see that, but I should have thought that teaching

the same thing over and over again to a new lot of children would become monotonous."

"They're all different. Of course it's true that the moment they begin to take a real interest in their work, the moment that you can really begin to educate them, they leave school. It's heartbreaking sometimes."

"Sometimes?"

"Not always by any means," declared Miss Carlyle with a little laugh. "Sometimes I must admit I'm glad to see the last of them. They vary in a most astonishing way—some so intelligent, others hopeless."

"What do you mean by hopeless?"

Miss Carlyle hesitated and then said, "I'm thinking of one particular child. She's nearly fourteen, leaving school at the end of this term, and she's practically illiterate. It's appalling, isn't it? I've failed with her. Or at least I've failed with her as regards lessons. Just lately she has improved a good deal in her personal appearance. I suppose that's something to be thankful for."

"Is she mentally deficient?" asked Kate.

"No, she wouldn't be with me if she were. She's quite normal in some ways—in every way except that I haven't been able to teach her to read or write. I've had her for four years, ever since I came to Old Quinings, and I've done my level best. Of course she has missed a good deal of schooling one way and another, but I *do* feel it's a most extraordinary case. Botany is the only subject in which she takes the slightest interest. She likes botany and often brings flowers and herbs to school and asks me their names. She remembers them, too. She never forgets what I tell her. You would think with a memory like that she could not help picking up a little—even just sitting in class and hearing the others and looking at the blackboard. She's neither deaf nor blind." Miss Carlyle laughed ruefully and shook her head.

"You can't get at her through her parents?" suggested Kate.

"Lily has no parents," said Miss Carlyle. "She lives

with her grandfather, a curious little man. To tell you the truth, Lily's grandfather reminds me of a gnome—the queer creatures described by Paracelsus. If you remember, he said gnomes move through the soil as fish move through water, without resistance, and leave no trace of their passing. They live and move and have their being in earth, they even breathe earth——"

"Abijah Rannish!" exclaimed Kate.

Miss Carlyle looked at her in surprise. "How did you know?" she asked.

"How could I not know?" laughed Kate. "There can't be two gnomes in Old Quinings."

They discussed Abijah and agreed that they did not like him; but Miss Carlyle asserted that Abijah was not altogether bad; he was devoted to Lily, declared Miss Carlyle. Kate was forced to admit that devotion to his granddaughter was a human and natural sentiment, but added that she was surprised to hear of anything human and natural about Abijah.

Having discussed Abijah thoroughly, Kate changed the subject to one which she hoped would be more fruitful. "What a splendid reference library Mr. Morven has!" she said.

"Yes," said Miss Carlyle briefly.

"Does he ever lend them to any one? I mean, would he——" She paused.

Miss Carlyle did not reply at once, and Kate, looking at her, saw her blush slowly right up to the roots of her hair. "Oh," said Miss Carlyle in a flustered manner. "Oh, yes, he does. He's very kind. I mean I'm sure he would if you asked him. Of course I can't—can't avail myself of—of that any more. I shall have to make—make some excuse——"

"Miss Carlyle!" exclaimed Richard Morven. The other three had stopped and were waiting on the path. Mr. Morven had a yellow flower in his hand. "Miss Carlyle, you're such a dab at botany. I'm sure you'll be able to tell us the name of this wild-flower. Mrs. Dove wants to know and I can't tell her."

"Ragwort," said Miss Carlyle. "It's of the *genus Senecio*, a most obnoxious weed. I feel sure your gardener dislikes it intensely."

They all laughed. Kate was surprised at the rapidity with which Miss Carlyle had recovered her composure, and of course she wondered what had caused her to lose it. But there was no chance of finding out at the moment, for having stopped and chatted it was natural for a reshuffle to take place. Kate found herself walking in front with her host. She was quite pleased, of course, or would have been pleased if her curiosity had not been aroused by Miss Carlyle's odd behaviour. Kate was slightly *distrait*, wondering about it, and failed to notice that her companion was hurrying her along. It was not until he opened a door in a high wall, ushered her into an enclosed garden, and shut the door firmly behind him, that Kate realised they had lost the rest of the party.

"Thank heaven!" he exclaimed. "I had to see you alone for a minute, Kate. You don't mind, do you?"

"No, of course not, Richard," replied Kate, smiling at him. It was the first time he had used her name and it sounded quite natural, for amongst her friends it was the usual thing—in fact she scarcely knew any one who called her Miss Hardy.

"I had to see you alone," repeated Richard. "I've heard from Wanda. She's in London. I don't know what on earth to do."

Kate sat down on a bench which was placed in a sunny corner near the door. She said, "It depends what you want to do, doesn't it?"

"I don't know," he declared, frowning. "I want to see her—and yet I don't. Kate, I know she came to see you at the Dower House. Mrs. Haygarth told me . . . nothing that happens in this place can be kept dark."

"I didn't want to keep it dark. In fact I saw no reason for it. Why shouldn't she come to see me if she wanted to?"

"Why should she!" Richard exclaimed.

Kate did not answer that. She said, " I'm very glad you know about it because I don't like secrets. I thought she was beautiful, Richard. I liked her."

" Why did she come ? What did she say ? "

" I don't think I can tell you that. What a pity Mrs. Haygarth didn't listen at the keyhole ! "

" Kate, you little devil ! " exclaimed Richard, laughing somewhat mirthlessly.

" It was a private matter," declared Kate. " It was a matter between Wanda and me and doesn't affect the question of whether or not you want a divorce."

" Does she want it ? "

" You must ask her. Honestly, Richard, I don't want to betray Wanda's confidence. In fact I refuse to do so."

Richard walked up and down twice. " You're right, of course," he said. " It has nothing at all to do with you— nothing. I shouldn't have asked. The fact is I'm upset about the whole thing. I must go and see Weller about it ; he will advise me what to do. You must keep out of it altogether. That's *essential*, Kate. *You* must on no account be involved."

Kate was silent. She knew exactly what he meant. He was telling her as clearly as he could under the circumstances that if he managed to obtain a divorce he would have something important to say to her. She liked him immensely . . . but it was no use thinking about it now. Kate decided not to think about it. She looked up at the trees. She said, " I'm afraid you may be a little annoyed with me. I have a confession to make. I've invited your daughter to come and stay at the Dower House."

" Susan ! " he exclaimed. " You've invited Susan——"

" It sounds queer, I know," admitted Kate. " It sounds interfering ; but I didn't mean it like that. Wanda is going to Switzerland and didn't know what to do with Susan, so I said I would have her. I'd have done the same thing for any child. There's no need for you to see Susan unless you want to."

" Of course I must see her," said Richard, frowning at

the ground. " People would think it most extraordinary . . ."

" But you don't want to."

" I see you think it's strange," Richard said. " The fact is I had a bit of a shock the other day ; I got an anonymous letter (a disgusting, ill-written, ill-spelt thing) saying that Susan was not my child, or words to that effect. It's quite within the bounds of possibility, of course. That's what makes it so—insidious."

" *You* got one ! " exclaimed Kate.

" Yes, I had never got such a thing before. It revolted me. I threw it into the fire, intending to put the whole thing out of my mind and take no notice of it. But I *can't*," declared Richard, driving his heel into the gravel as he spoke. " I just simply can't put it out of my mind. I keep thinking about it, and wondering. I wish now I hadn't burnt the wretched thing. I might have discovered who wrote it and whether there was any truth in it——"

At this moment (while Kate was still debating the matter and trying to decide whether to tell Richard about the anonymous letter which Wanda had received and which, more likely than not, had been written by the same untruthful pen) the door in the wall opened and the other three appeared.

" Oh, there you are ! " cried Milly. " We couldn't think where you'd gone."

" It looked so odd," declared Milly as they walked home through the woods. " It really was extraordinary of you, Kate. I mean the way you rushed off with Mr. Morven and left us all behind. Minta and I know you, of course, so we weren't surprised—I mean you do these sort of things without thinking—but I could see Miss Carlyle thought your behaviour *most odd*, and I must say I didn't blame her."

Kate made no reply. If she said anything she would say too much—and what was the use of quarrelling. It was curious how Milly had the power, by a few ill-chosen words, to raise such an unholy storm of rage in her sister's bosom.

CHAPTER FIFTEEN

On Monday morning Martha took a tray of morning tea to Mrs. Dove's bedroom (it was a luxury, of course, but Mrs. Dove was a visitor at the Dower House and visitors are entitled to special consideration). She found Mrs. Dove awake and in a complaining mood. A cock had wakened her at goodness knows what time, and a cow, " mooing," had prevented her from going to sleep again.

" It's *much* noisier here than in town," said Milly pettishly. " How can you *bear* it, Martha ? "

" I'm strong," said Martha dryly. " I can bear most things if I get my food."

" Martha, wouldn't you like to come back ? " said Milly, raising herself on her pillows.

" I'm well enough as I am," replied Martha.

" I would pay you higher wages. I would give you— well, I would give you *more* than you're getting from Miss Kate."

Martha stood and looked at her grimly. Mrs. Dove was silly, of course, so she did not realise how " low " that was. Bribery, thought Martha, looking at her.

" I would really," said Milly, rushing upon her fate.

" I dare say you would," declared Martha, " but I couldn't serve a person if I didn't respect them, and that's the truth."

" Oh, dear, I wish you would," said Milly, ignoring or possibly not even perceiving the frightful insult which had been offered her (it ran off her like water off a duck's back, Martha thought). " I do wish you would. I am *so* miserable, Martha. It's so *lonely* without any one to talk to. Minta is out all day and often most of the night . . . sometimes I can't help *crying* when I think of how lonely and wretched I am."

It was true, of course. Martha realised that it was true

H

and felt quite sorry for her in spite of the fact that her sad condition was entirely her own fault. She was a poor shilpit creature, thought Martha, pityingly. Aloud she said, " I thought you might find it a wee bit dull."

This from Martha was real sympathy (for Martha's habit of under-statement amounted to a vice), and Milly, recognising it as such, was encouraged to continue her lament. " It's frightful," wailed Milly. " It's absolutely *appalling*. Hour after hour goes by and there's nobody to talk to, nobody at *all* . . . and look at my *hands* ! Just *look* at my hands, Martha, and they used to be so *nice* ! I used to be so proud of my hands and now I have to *hide* them if any one looks at them."

" It's the hard water," said Martha.

" I *know*, but what can I *do* ? The dishes have *got* to be washed and I can't get any help at all. I can't hear of *any one* . . . and I'm so *exhausted*, standing on my feet all day, cooking. I'm so exhausted that I'm too paralysed to *speak*. I'm just absolutely dead to the *world*."

" M'ph'm," said Martha. " Cooking's apt to be a wee bit tiring when you're not used to it."

There was a short silence.

" I wonder," said Milly at last in a thoughtful voice. " Of course I know Miss Kate only asked us to come for the week-end . . ."

" Just from Saturday to Monday," said Martha, nodding

". . . but you see Minta is going to Chester to-day for a short visit ; so if I went back to town I should be all by myself, shouldn't I ? "

" That's so," agreed Martha.

" I wonder if I could stay on here for a few days longer ? '

" You'd need to ask Miss Kate."

" Oh, yes, of course, but I wondered what she would say."

" Why not ask her and see ? "

" Of course Miss Kate knows I don't like the country much. I mean that's why she only asked us for the week-end. Isn't it ? "

" I couldn't say, I'm sure."

" I wouldn't bother her at *all*," declared Milly. " I mean she could go on with her writing just as if I wasn't here. I should be quite happy to *rest*."

Martha did not reply to this. It needed no reply. " You'd best stay in bed to your breakfast anyway. That'll give you a wee rest," said Martha, and so saying she left Mrs. Dove to enjoy her morning tea and went to waken Miss Kate.

Kate was asleep and dreaming. It was a pleasant dream. She was in a ship floating down a broad estuary with meadows and woodlands on either side, and with her were Stephen and Walter and Francis Drake. They were all quite real to Kate, three men with different personalities . . . and then somehow they fused together and became one man, standing in the prow of the ship, gazing towards the sea.

". . . and by his light
Did all the chivalry of England move
To do brave acts."

These words came into Kate's mind and she woke murmuring them softly. She woke slowly and peacefully and saw Martha. Dear old Martha ; there was no need to talk. Kate smiled at her lazily.

" It's not often you're asleep when I waken you," said Martha and went away.

How curious it was to come back to real life after a dream, thought Kate, lying with her hands behind her head and considering the matter ; to come back to real life and personal responsibility. There is no personal responsibility in dreams. Things happen to us and we accept them ; we accept the impossible without surprise ; our critical faculties are asleep. We float . . . how heavenly that floating sensation ! We swim through the air, rising to the ceiling as easily and lightly as thistledown. Sometimes we go to strange places. Where have I been, thought Kate. Have

I really been there? Does that river exist, and, if so, how
do I know it to dream about it? If it does not exist, how
have I dreamt it? Have I imagined it? Have I made it
myself?

But all this, although intensely interesting, was getting
her nowhere. She had come back to real life and personal
responsibility. She was Kate Hardy again, and Kate Hardy
had to decide what her personal responsibility was in this
curious matter of Richard Morven and his wife and
daughter. She had been too tired and muddled to think
about it last night but she must think about it now. She
thought about it.

Richard had not actually said he wanted a divorce but
he had implied it, and, as Wanda wanted it too, they would
probably get it. Kate objected to divorce on principle, but
this case was unusual. It was a passionless affair. Here
were two people who were utterly unsuited to one another,
who liked different things, and enjoyed different kinds of
lives. It was impossible for them to live together happily,
so the sensible thing was to break the bond that bound
them together and go their different ways. Kate saw that
clearly. Her own part was to keep out of it and not inter-
fere—Richard had said so—but she could not keep out of
it altogether. She had got mixed up in it without meaning
to. There was Susan, for instance—or Lilias. (Would she
ever remember to call the child Lilias?) Perhaps Lilias
would not come, in which case things would be easier. It
had been a crazy impulse to ask Lilias to come. Quite crazy,
said Kate to herself. Richard was annoyed, and she could
not blame him, especially after the anonymous letter he had
received. It would be most uncomfortable to have the
child here, with Richard coming in, as he so often did. It
would be uncomfortable for Richard to see the child . . .
and wonder about her.

" I'm in for a gorgeous time," said Kate to herself.

This brought Kate to her second problem (or was it
her third?), the problem of the anonymous letter. Should
she tell Richard about the anonymous letter which Wanda

had received, the utterly disgusting missive which had brought Wanda, hot foot, from America? She did not want to tell him, for obvious reasons, and she had decided there was no need to tell him; but now that Richard had received a letter of the same mischievous nature perhaps she ought to tell him. For one thing the author of these effusions should be traced and silenced, and, for another, it would relieve Richard's mind to know he was not the only victim of the poison pen. Wanda's letter had contained false information, so it was probable that Richard's letter was equally untrue to fact.

Kate decided, most reluctantly, that Richard must be told.

When Kate went down to breakfast she found Minta enjoying a boiled egg. Minta was going to Chester this morning, so she was dressed ready for the journey and looked smart and sophisticated in black, with a small black hat perched at a ridiculous angle upon her curls. She was a pretty creature, thought her aunt, and an attractive creature . . . if only Milly did not spoil her so outrageously.

"How I adore eggs!" said Minta. "Country eggs! They're utterly and absolutely different from the town variety. Are they laid by a different kind of fowl?"

"Could you eat another?" inquired her hostess.

"Try me," said Minta with a grin.

Kate ordered another egg and sat down to eat her porridge and open her mail.

"May I open some of the 'fans,'" asked Minta. "They amuse me no end. Here's one from America, Aunt Kate."

"Open them all," replied the author, who, it is to be feared, was just a trifle *blasé* about her fan-mail.

"This is from Chicago," declared Minta, her utterance slightly impeded by a large mouthful of toast. "This man says he likes your books, and Stephen is a real guy, but he wishes you would be more careful with your facts. Stephen couldn't have dressed in three minutes—so this man says. He tried it himself and it just isn't possible."

"I can," said Kate. "Pass the marmalade, please. I tried it to see."

"But you aren't a man, darling. I mean men have buttons and things, haven't they? Why had poor Stephen so little time? Oh, Aunt Kate, listen to this! Here's a girl who's dying to meet you. Stephen is her *beau ideal* and she feels sure he's a self-portrait of his author. There's reams all about her history *and* a photograph and she wants one of you in return. Aunt Kate, I believe she wants to marry you!"

"Of course," said Kate, nodding. "Quite a lot of girls do."

"Poor souls!" exclaimed Minta, laying the letter aside. "Oh, here's a good one—or isn't it? Here's a woman who has read all your books and hopes you'll write another in time for Christmas as she wants to send it to her uncle, who is bedridden. You couldn't refuse that request, could you?"

"I could quite easily," retorted Kate, "and even supposing I were to grant it I doubt if my publishers would rush the book into print."

"Not for a bedridden uncle?"

"Not for twenty bedridden uncles," declared Kate.

"She adores your books," declared Minta, scanning the closely-written pages. "She absolutely dotes on Steven— with a 'v.' If she dotes so devotedly you would think she could spell his name."

"No, I wouldn't, really," replied the author. "I had a letter the other day from a girl who said she loved Mark."

"Amazing!" declared Minta. "Of course it is the same *sort* of name, but why write at all if you're as vague as that? Better to save the stamp. By the way, can I have this American stamp? There's a picture of dear Roosevelt on it . . . Gerald collects stamps."

"Gerald?"

"One of my boy friends, darling; the very latest. He's a pet . . . and talking of boy friends," said Minta (whose conversation was apt to run on in this chain-like manner),

" talking of boy friends, I'm pretty certain mother's out to pinch yours."

" What *do* you mean ? "

" Mr. Morven," said Minta nodding. " darling mother is on the war-path, so you'd better look out. She sees herself as Lady of the Manor, dispensing soup and blankets to curtseying cottagers and soothing the pillows of the indigent sick. I thought I ought to warn you ; it doesn't seem very fair."

Kate laughed cheerfully. She said, " My dear lamb, he isn't my boy friend, and, even if he were, a boy friend who can be pinched so easily isn't worth having."

Minta rose and lighted a cigarette. " Well, that's O.K.," she said.

" Besides," added Kate, " your mother is going back to town this afternoon."

" Not if she knows it," said Minta.

Kate was still speechless with the shock of this announcement when the telephone bell rang. She picked up the receiver and heard a voice say, " This is a telegram for Hardy, Old Quinings 44, handed in at Mayfair 8.45. The message is : *Lilias arriving three-fifty this afternoon Wanda.* Do you want a confirmation ? "

" No, thank you," said Kate putting back the receiver.

" What on earth was it ? " inquired Minta. " You look as if somebody had offered you a scorpion."

" I feel exactly like that," replied Kate.

CHAPTER SIXTEEN

SHE WAS a leggy child, coltish and awkward. Kate, who had gone to meet her at the station, saw her get out of the train and stand on the platform looking about her with a curiously eager gaze. She had a long neck and sloping shoulders, accentuated by a long green coat, loosely cut. She had no hat and the sun shone upon the fuzzy fair hair which surrounded her face like a bush. There was something rather pathetic about the child, thought Kate as she hurried to greet her guest.

" Here you are, Susan ! " cried Kate.

" You're Miss Hardy, I suppose."

They shook hands gravely and walked towards the taxi, which was waiting.

" I'm sorry," said Kate as they got in. " I should have called you Lilias, shouldn't I ? "

" Susan is my name," replied the child.

Kate accepted the fact without comment. She was relieved to find she need not remember to call her guest Lilias ; besides, it would make things a good deal easier where Richard was concerned. Richard could not be expected to understand the reason for the change (it was the crazy sort of thing that no man could be expected to understand) and the discovery that his daughter—if she were his daughter—had seen fit to discard his mother's name would not help to endear her to him.

Their drive from the station was comparatively silent, for Kate had decided to go slow until she began to understand the problem-child and Susan apparently saw no need for conversation. Susan sat forward on the seat and gazed out of the somewhat dirty window, taking in everything she saw.

" But I don't remember it at all ! " she said suddenly.

" You were just a baby, weren't you ? "

" I thought I would remember a *little*," said Susan with a sigh.

In one way Kate was disappointed in her guest : she had hoped Susan would look like Richard or at least bear some resemblance to him. It would have helped a lot if Kate could have said, " The child has got your eyes " or " Susan's hands are the same shape as yours, aren't they ? " But try as she might Kate could find nothing of Richard in the child. There was nothing of Wanda either; except, perhaps, the way she spoke. In another way Kate was agreeably surprised, for Susan seemed good and quiet and showed none of the peculiarities which her mother had deplored. Kate had only very muddled ideas as to what sort of behaviour she might expect, for Wanda had been extremely vague about it and had contradicted herself frequently ; saying first of all that " Lilias " was very, very difficult and absolutely unmanageable, and in the next breath that " Lilias " was really not much bother, unless you got up against her, in which case she was apt to let herself go ; assuring Miss Hardy that she would scarcely notice the child was in the house, and adding that of course when " Lilias " really got going she could raise the roof. No wonder Kate was surprised and pleased when she beheld this bag of trouble sitting upon the sofa in the drawing-room and reading *Alice in Wonderland* with rapt attention. Milly was not so surprised, for she had not been warned of what they might expect from their newly-arrived guest.

At supper special food had been provided according to the *régime*—parts of which had stuck in Kate's mind. There was lemonade for Susan to drink, and steamed fish with parsley sauce and salad for her to eat, all neatly laid out upon a tray ; but Susan refused these comestibles and ate macaroni and cheese and drank coffee like her elders. Kate was worried, of course, but the child was so polite and sensible that she did not know what to do. One could hardly compel one's guest to eat food she did not fancy, especially when one would not have fancied it oneself.

After supper Susan returned to the sofa and *Alice*. She

had not read the book before—a surprising matter to Kate who had been brought up on it; but Susan explained this by saying Dr. Schneider didn't approve of fairy tales, and continued to absorb it avidly. It was a little difficult for Kate. Obviously her duty was to remove the book forthwith; but *could* she, without risking a scene; and after all, was it conceivable that the story of Alice's adventures could do any one any harm?

Wanda had decreed that her daughter must go to bed at eight. This, at least, was wise. It was the only sensible part of the *régime* in Kate's opinion . . . but when the clock struck eight and Kate suggested bed, the suggestion was met with a refusal.

" No, thank you," said Susan politely. She turned over a page and read on.

" Yes, Susan," said Kate. " You've had a long day and you must be tired."

" No," said Susan, without raising her head.

" While you're in this house you must do as you're told."

Susan looked up. " I never do as I'm told—unless I want to," said Susan frankly. " It isn't good for me, Dr. Schneider says. I'm a very nervous child, you see. I'm terribly highly strung."

Kate was appalled. For a few moments she was speechless with dismay at the implications of this announcement; and then she pulled herself together. This was the test, thought Kate. If she couldn't make Susan go to bed now, she would never be able to make Susan do anything. The idea was unpleasant to say the least of it, for the child was in her charge. Could she carry Susan to bed, wondered Kate, eyeing Susan doubtfully.

" All little girls go to bed at eight," declared Milly. She was knitting a bed-jacket in pink wool and did not bother to raise her eyes. " It may be different in America, of course; I don't know, because I haven't been there, but in England *all* little girls go to bed at eight."

Susan rose at once. She tucked her book under her arm and went up to bed like a lamb.

"You see," said Milly smugly, "children are *so* easy to manage if you go about it the right way! The great thing is to show them you won't stand any nonsense; to be kind but firm."

Kate saw, or thought she saw, the inner truth of the matter: the reason why Milly had succeeded where she had failed. If she were right, it was going to be fairly easy to control Susan and guide her in the way she should go.

The evening passed quietly and at ten o'clock Kate went into the kitchen to say good-night to Martha before going upstairs. She found Martha in an unusually talkative mood, eager to discuss the idiosyncracies of the new arrival.

"She's a caution and no mistake," declared Martha. "Nice manners, she has, I *will* say that. I unpacked her things for her and she thanked me quite nicely. All green, they are, Miss Kate."

Kate had expected her things to be all green, so she was not surprised.

"*All* green, Miss Kate," repeated Martha. "Even to her very semmits—green as grass. Would that be an America custom, do you suppose?"

Kate thought not. It was quite an alarming idea to conceive of a hundred and twenty-two million people all wearing green next the skin.

"She calls her mother Wanda," continued Martha in scandalised tones. "That's a funny thing if you like. Where's the respect in that, Miss Kate?"

"I don't think it means very much," said Kate smiling. "Perhaps Mrs. Morven prefers it. She's young and pretty, you know."

Martha took the point. "Well, if she likes it that's all right," said Martha doubtfully. "It wouldn't suit me."

"It wouldn't suit me either, Martha. I think I had better tell Susan to call me 'Aunt Kate;' don't you?"

"You'll do as you please, of course," said Martha in her usual uncompromising way. "She called you Miss Hardy to me, but there's no saying what she might take it into her head to do. I doubt we'll need to buy her some sort of hat."

" Some sort of hat ! " echoed Kate, surprised at this sudden change of subject.

" M'ph'm," nodded Martha. " The child hasn't a hat to her name—not even a tammy. I said to her, ' Have you no hat, Susan ? It's a funny thing to go a railway journey without a hat,' and she said she had one when she started but she threw it out of the window. Can you beat that, Miss Kate ? I told her it was naughty," continued Martha in serious tones. " I said to her, ' That's not funny, Susan ! that's a naughty thing to do. You're a bad wee girl to do a thing like that.' ' Oh, no,' says she, as calm as a cucumber. ' It was just a natural impulse. It's very bad for me to control my natural impulses.' "

" I hope you told her she would have to control them while she was here," suggested Kate.

" I did my best," replied Martha. " I reasoned with the creature. I told her I'd never heard such talk in all my born days, but I doubt I was wasting my breath. Believe me, Miss Kate, that child has never been taught the difference between good and bad."

" She's been to all sorts of doctors," explained Kate, who was anxious that her new charge should stand well with Martha. " They have pulled her about and talked about her in front of her, which is always a mistake. When Susan says these extraordinary things she's just quoting what she's overheard the doctors say."

Martha looked thoughtful. " That's as may be," she said. " But all the same she's got some queer notions in her head. I'll need to take her to church . . . it's a pity there's not a sensible Presbyterian minister in the place with a good sound knowledge of doctrine. Mr. Barton is nice enough in his way—I'm not saying anything against him—but he's not what you'd call a very convincing preacher. You should have heard Dr. Ferguson, Miss Kate. I tell you, when he got onto the subject of hell he fairly made your blood run cold."

CHAPTER SEVENTEEN

KATE had neglected Stephen for several days ; in fact she had not written a word since Saturday—and to-day was Tuesday. She explained to her guests at breakfast that she intended to write all the morning, and her guests assured her that they understood the position and would amuse themselves. Susan had been told by Martha that Miss Hardy was the author of the Slade Books and was quite overcome by this disclosure. She had read two of them, and was eager to start the third when she had finished *Alice's Adventures in Wonderland*.

" But you don't understand them, dear," said Milly in reproving tones. " The Slade Books are for grown-up people ; they aren't meant for little girls."

" You've got a nerve ! " exclaimed Susan in disgust. " I'm just as clever as you are, but I'll go on getting cleverer and you'll stay the same—that's the difference between us."

This was so true that Kate was speechless (Milly also was speechless, though not for the same reason), but Susan still had plenty to say.

" Stephen is marvellous," declared Susan in a dreamy voice. " Stephen is the most marvellous man in the world. Nobody else could have caught Savernake—nobody else realised that Savernake was a crook . . ." and she continued to discuss Stephen's activities in a manner which showed she had not only read but inwardly digested every word of the Slade Books.

" Does Dr. Schneider approve of them ? " inquired the author with interest as she rose and gathered up her letters and prepared to leave the room.

" He doesn't know everything," replied Susan darkly.

By this time Milly had recovered her powers of speech. It was obvious that she was making a superhuman effort to be a perfect guest.

" You must have a long quiet morning, Kate," declared Milly. " I'll do the shopping and Susan can come with me and help to carry the basket. You needn't worry about us at all."

Susan neither accepted nor refused. She had a wary look.

Kate went into the morning-room and sat down at her desk. She began to think about Stephen. It was not easy to get back into the atmosphere of her book after the excitements of the last few days, but she made a determined effort, and was just beginning to rekindle the flame when Martha looked in.

" Miss Kate," said Martha, " I thought I'd just catch you before you started. Walter Stack has come. Did you want him to make shelves in the attic ? "

" Yes ! " cried Kate, leaping to her feet. This was one of her dearest projects—shelves in the attic for apples and pears—so she did not resent the interruption to her work ; to be truthful she welcomed it. She ran upstairs and found Walter in the attic measuring the wall.

" This is splendid ! " exclaimed Kate. " I was afraid Mr. Seager had put you on to another job."

" I've just enough wood left, I think," said Walter, pointing to the remains of the partition which was leaning against the wall. " There's some junk in the corner ; I might find some more wood there. I'll see, anyhow."

Kate glanced into the dark corner. " None of that is mine," she said. " But I don't suppose Mr. Morven wants it or he would have taken it away."

They decided where the shelves were to go and measured the wood. Walter took off his jacket, put on his overalls and started work. Kate sat down on a large wooden chest and watched him. It was interesting to watch Walter. He was so sure ; he wasted no time ; he knew exactly what he was doing.

" Aren't you writing this morning ? " asked Walter.

" I should be," replied Kate. " This is just—laziness."

" I haven't said anything about your books," said Walter, talking as he worked. " It isn't because I don't like them, it's because I like them so much. I feel whatever I could say would be—would be insufficient."

"I'd rather you didn't say anything," declared Kate hastily.

"But I *would* like to tell you one thing," said Walter, stopping work for a few moments and looking at her. "I would just like to tell you that when we were in the jungle, stripped to the bare minimum of kit (which consisted of a knapsack one had to carry oneself) I had Stephen Slade with me. He and Izaak Walton journeyed together in the knapsack—rather an odd couple, but most carefully chosen, I can tell you."

"Oh!" said Kate in a low voice. "Oh, Walter, that's the very nicest thing——"

"And now I'll tell you something that you won't like nearly so much," said Walter, smiling. "*I knew Kenneth Hardy was a woman.*"

"You knew? How on earth did you know that? Everybody says——"

"I thought you might be angry," chuckled Walter.

"I'm not angry. Tell me how you knew."

"I read the book very carefully, of course," admitted Walter. "I don't suppose many of your readers are reduced to two books——"

"Tell me quickly," urged Kate, interrupting him.

"Very few men blow out the match when they've lighted their pipe," said Walter.

"They shake it out!" cried Kate after a moment's thought.

"Exactly."

Kate was silent for a little and then she inquired meekly, "Was there anything else?"

Walter nodded. "Stephen hadn't shaved for three days—you remember, it was when he was hiding from Savernake in the ruined mill—then he managed to get hold of a razor 'and in a few minutes he was himself again.' Gosh!" said Walter, feeling his chin and smiling ruefully. "Three days beard gone in a few minutes . . . and the fellow hadn't even hot water and soap!"

"Oh, Walter!" exclaimed the author in horrified tones.

" Oh, goodness, how frightfully silly of me ! I knew that, of course—about the soap and water. Why on earth was I such a fool ! "

" You knew it with your mind. If you had been a man you'd have known it in your bones. No man *could* have made that mistake . . . It was interesting," continued Walter, measuring a piece of wood and marking it with his pencil. " It was really tremendously interesting. When I had made up my mind that Kenneth Hardy was a woman in disguise I read the book again, more carefully than before, and I saw, or imagined I saw, the woman's point of view peeping out in several places. Or, to put it differently, I saw a point of view which was certainly not that of an average man. I saw other things too. You can't read a book as carefully as that without getting to know the author . . . so when I met you I felt I knew you already."

" We were friends," nodded Kate. " That very first night we were friends. I felt it, too. I'm so glad, Walter."

Kate had wasted more than half an hour of her precious morning. Perhaps " wasted " was not quite the right word, but still . . . She went downstairs, sat down at her desk and seized her pen. The last words she had written stared at her from the page.

" *Stephen seized his hat and ran out of* . . ."

Kate was about to complete the sentence—it was not difficult to complete—when there was a gentle knock on the door.

" Kate," said Milly, looking in, " Kate, I won't disturb you, but Martha and I are a little fussed. You see, I'm all ready to go to the village and Martha has given me the list, but we can't find Susan anywhere."

" Go without her," said Kate.

" I suppose she'll be all *right*," said Milly doubtfully.

" Perfectly all right," said Kate.

" She isn't in the house *or* garden."

" She'll be all right," said Kate.

The door closed very softly and Kate heaved a sigh of relief. She completed the unfinished sentence and then paused . . . Of *course* Susan would be all right. What could happen to her in Old Quinings? *Nothing* could happen to her. "Nothing?" inquired an annoying imp in Kate's mind. "Are you sure? She might go out on to the road and be run over . . . vehicles drive on the right in America. You know that. She might have wandered onto the moor . . . She might get lost, mightn't she?"

"Oh, damn!" cried Kate aloud. "I'm going to write this morning! Two women ought to be enough to look after one child."

She began to write laboriously, crossing out every other sentence and rewriting it in different words. When she had finished a page she read it over and tore it up into small pieces.

At this moment Martha opened the door and, tiptoeing across the room, laid an envelope on Kate's desk.

"Martha," said Kate, "it disturbs me far more when you come in like that than if you opened the door with a crash and clumped in with clogs on your feet."

Martha was speechless at this ingratitude.

"And what's *this*," continued Kate irritably, taking up the envelope and looking at it. "Is it the butcher's bill or what?"

"Oh, Miss Kate, you know I wouldn't disturb you if *that* was all it was!"

Kate tore the note open. The message read: "*Would it be possible for me to see you for a few minutes? Anne Carlyle.*"

"Yes, I'll see her," said Kate with a sigh.

Miss Carlyle came in. "This is very good of you, Miss Hardy," she said. "It really *is* important or I wouldn't have bothered you. I mustn't stay more than a few minutes; the children are having their eleven o'clock break."

"Come and sit down," said Kate, who saw that Miss Carlyle was worried and upset. "Come and tell me about it."

"Thank you," said Miss Carlyle. "The fact is I don't know what to do, and you were so kind and understanding. I very nearly told you on Sunday, but we were interrupted.

Perhaps you don't remember. We were talking about Mr.
Morven's library."

Kate remembered, and all the more clearly because she
now saw the same phenomenon take place before her eyes :
Miss Carlyle blushed.

" Oh, dear, I am foolish," declared Miss Carlyle. " But
this has upset me dreadfully. Nothing of this sort has ever
happened to me before. It is so horrible and degrading
that—that I hardly know how to tell you."

" An anonymous letter, I suppose," said Kate.

. " How did you know ! " exclaimed Miss Carlyle in
amazement.

" You're the third," Kate told her. " The third I've
heard of—there may be others, of course."

" Then I'm not the only victim ! "

Kate looked at her and she saw she was pleased. It
seemed odd in a way, but in another way it was not unnatural, for only a most unselfish person would prefer to bear
misfortune alone.

" It was a short message," said Miss Carlyle, glancing
at the clock. " Quite short and extremely illiterate. It
commented on the fact that I visit the Manor frequently
and drew erroneous conclusions. As I told you, Mr. Morven
allows me to borrow his books and I have his permission
to go in and out without troubling the Haygarths. I've
also done a little typing for Mr. Morven—business letters
and that sort of thing. It's a businees arrangement, a matter
of mutual convenience. He gives me the run of his library
and I'm useful to him in a secretarial capacity . . . and
how glad I am to be able to help him ! "

" Yes, of course."

" Now everything is spoilt. I can't go back to the
Manor. It will be the greatest deprivation. I don't know
what Mr. Morven will think when he finds I've stopped
going . . . and what makes me just as unhappy is the
knowledge that someone has misjudged my motives so
radically. The accusation that I am *after Mr. Morven* fills
me with shame. Who could have written it ? "

" Perhaps a child——" began Kate.

" A child ! " cried Miss Carlyle in horrified tones.
" Surely not a child ! What child would know or care about
such things ? "

" A person pretending to be illiterate, then ? " asked
Kate, remembering that this was Wanda's suggestion.

" No," replied Miss Carlyle. " No, it isn't that. A
person who pretends to be illiterate nearly always spells
the wrong words wrongly—if you know what I mean. I have
a good deal of experience in the matter and I feel sure the
message was written by an individual who can neither write
nor spell except in a deplorably illiterate way."

Kate was willing to take her word for it.

" But what I came to ask you is this : Must I take it
to the police ? Is it my duty, Miss Hardy ? "

" I don't know," said Kate thoughtfully. " I suppose
it is the right thing to do, but I think I should be inclined
to wait a little. It would be very unpleasant for you to take
it to the police, wouldn't it ? "

" I can't imagine anything I should dislike more,"
declared Miss Carlyle.

There was a short silence.

" Things are very difficult for me just now," said Miss
Carlyle, rising to go. " They say troubles never come singly.
There's something odd going on in school and I can't put
my finger on it . . . but I won't trouble you with that."

" Something odd ? " inquired Kate, who objected to
having her curiosity aroused and left unsatisfied.

" Yes. Just lately the children have been—not exactly
troublesome, I can deal with that—they have been inatten-
tive. They have been—yes—furtive. I don't like it at all.
At first I thought it was just—just the usual thing that one
has to look out for, especially in a place like this. But it isn't
that."

" Have you no clue at all ? " asked Kate. They were
both standing now. Miss Carlyle was on the point of
departure.

" Not really," she replied. " They've begun to play a

silly game—it seems quite pointless. They always used to play Prisoners' Base during their eleven o'clock break. Now they play this—not all of them, of course, but a biggish group—they stand in a ring and pick handfuls of grass and throw it over their heads."

"They're playing witches, I think."

There was a short silence and then Kate added, " I don't mean the sort of witches you read of in fairy tales——"

" I know you don't," interrupted Miss Carlyle. " *That* wouldn't matter, *this* does. I know a good deal about the subject, because I've always been tremendously interested in the rural history of England . . . Witches ! " said Miss Carlyle in a horrified tone. " Yes, it fits in rather horribly with other things. Some of the children have been suffering from nightmares and their parents have complained. I shall have to stop it, that's all. I don't *like* stopping things, you know, because so often it doesn't really stop them but only drives them underground, where they're even more difficult to deal with."

" It will make it seem more important if you stop it."

Miss Carlyle nodded and picked up her gloves. " Oh, dear," she said. " This makes my own little trouble seem rather unimportant." She hesitated and added, " You've been so kind. I wish you would call me Anne," and with that she went away.

Kate sat down at her desk. It was quite impossible to write. Her mind was full of other things. She sat there for some minutes thinking about Miss Carlyle's two problems. They seemed unrelated . . . but, coming at the same moment, Kate felt there must be a link. What could the link be ?

The door opened and Milly's face appeared. She said, " Kate, don't stop writing. I just looked in to tell you Susan has come back *quite* safely."

" Has she ? " said Kate.

" Quite safely," said Milly, nodding. " She's upstairs in the attic watching the man putting up shelves. She's as good as gold."

"Is she?" said Kate.

"I was afraid you might be worrying, so I thought I would just look in and tell you it was all right. I haven't disturbed you, have I?"

"No," said Kate.

Milly shut the door with elaborate care.

CHAPTER EIGHTEEN

THE NEXT few days were fairly peaceful. Susan behaved like a reasonable being except occasionally when she "let herself go." She was bilingual, which is to say that she spoke cultured English and low American slang with equal facility. It was a little disconcerting at times and at other times amusing . . . instructive, too, thought Kate. It was both amusing and instructive when Susan was asked if she knew where Mrs. Dove happened to be and replied shortly, "Guess she's sitting on the back of her neck in the lounge." This description of Milly's reposeful attitude was graphic in the extreme. It was not quite so funny when Susan became annoyed with Martha and implored her to stop shooting her mouth off, or when she informed Mrs. Stack that she was a pain in the neck. On the whole, however, Susan was good; her hostess became deeply attached to her and at the same time very much disturbed about her future. She would return to America with her mother and be pulled about and prodded and poked at by every quack doctor Wanda could lay her hands on. What Susan needed was a quiet regular existence and a solid foundation for her feet. Her life had been such that she had lost the childish feeling of the permanence of people and things before she had found any other solid ground.

For a few days the little household was self-contained: neither Richard nor Anne Carlyle was seen; Walter had almost finished the shelves in the attic, and Kate had progressed with her book.

Mr. Barton called one morning. Kate liked him and enjoyed his sermons. so she put aside her work and received him cordially. He sat down on the sofa and talked about the weather and thanked Miss Hardy for delivering the magazines for his wife. Kate had a feeling that he had come to see her about something more important than the weather, and her suspicions were soon to be confirmed, for after a little silence Mr. Barton drew a deep breath and took the plunge.

" I've been thinking," said Mr. Barton, his thin æsthetic face becoming somewhat red with embarrassment. " You know, Miss Hardy, you have a tremendous power for good. Couldn't you use it more ? "

" You mean my books ? " said Kate in some bewilderment.

" Your books, of course," he replied. " They sell in thousands—so I'm told. You have a very wide public. Your books are delightful, if I may say so, very delightful indeed, but it seemed to me that you might make more use of your popularity. I preach to a couple of hundred people but you could preach to thousands," added Mr. Barton in earnest tones.

" I just amuse them——" Kate began.

" And most successfully," interrupted Mr. Barton eagerly. " It's because you're so successful that you could do so much good. You could bring religion to people who never go to church, couldn't you ? "

Kate looked at him and liked him immensely. He was so earnest, so sincere. " But my stories are not a suitable instrument to spread religion," objected Kate.

" They could be ! "

" I don't think so. People buy my books for entertainment, Mr. Barton. If I started to write tracts I should very soon have no public at all. Besides, I don't think I'm qualified to teach religion ; that's your job, isn't it ? "

His face fell. " But I wish you would try," he said. " I do wish it most earnestly."

During the short silence which followed Mr. Barton's

plea, Kate happened to glance at the window and saw Susan standing there. She signed to Susan to go away, but instead of obeying Susan leapt into the room. Her face was flushed and her eyes were flashing fire.

" I heard you, you big stuffed eel ! " cried Susan in ringing tones, pointing to Mr. Barton, so that there should be no doubt as to whom she was addressing. " I heard what you said ; but she's gotta go on writing about *Stephen*. So don't you go trying to gum up the works or you'll get what's coming to you ! "

Poor Mr. Barton gazed at this sudden apparition in alarm.

" Susan ! " cried Kate, struggling with a mixture of emotions amongst which shame and anger and laughter strove to gain the upper hand. " Susan, I'm surprised at you ! Go away at once. You had no business to listen . . ." Kate's voice broke off with a quiver ; sometimes a keen sense of humour is a disadvantage to its possessor.

Fortunately Mr. Barton had a sense of humour, too, and when he had recovered from his shock he began to laugh very heartily indeed. " Dear me," he said. " The American idiom is most graphic . . . quite alarmingly so . . ."

Kate rose and pushed Susan out of the door. She would deal with Susan later. " It's very good of you to take it like this, Mr. Barton," declared Kate. " I *do* apologise for Susan . . . I shall punish her, of course."

" Please don't be too severe," said Mr. Barton, mopping his eyes. " She has given us a good laugh and that should count in her favour ; besides, I feel Susan had just cause to be annoyed. The last thing I intended was to gum up the works."

He began to laugh again, and this time Kate, who had controlled herself with the utmost difficulty, joined in. No more serious conversation was possible after that, and Mr. Barton took his departure.

Kate did not look forward to punishing Susan ; in fact she had no idea how to set about it ; but something must be done. She could not overlook the fact that Susan had been eavesdropping and had been extremely rude into the bargain; so when Mr. Barton had gone and she had composed herself sufficiently, she called Susan into the morning-room and tried to bring home to her the enormity of her offence.

" But I wasn't listening to you talking," declared Susan, standing in the middle of the room and looking back at Kate with mutiny in her eyes. " I was trying *not* to listen. I was waiting until that old punk had gone to give you a message from Martha. Martha said I was to ask you for the key of the store cupboard directly he'd gone, so that it wouldn't be another interruption . . . and how could I know directly he'd gone unless I was there to see ? "

Kate was reasonable, she took the point. " But you were rude, Susan," she said. " It was terribly rude to interrupt us like that and to call Mr. Barton names."

" I called him a big stuffed eel and so he is ! " cried Susan, stamping her foot with rage. " Anybody who wants you to stop writing about Stephen is a stuffed eel."

" I was ashamed of you, Susan. And the silly thing about it is that you didn't understand. Mr. Barton never intended to—to——" Kate's voice quivered again.

" He said it, anyhow," declared Susan.

Kate left it at that. She could not trust herself to discuss it. " You were rude and naughty," she said. " If you want to stay here at the Dower House you mustn't be rude to my friends. I won't have it."

There was a short silence. It was rather an important moment, for Susan was weighing the merits of two different courses of action. Should she take these reproofs meekly or throw herself on the floor and scream ? Screaming had been her trump card in any little trouble which had arisen between herself and Wanda (for Wanda always gave in directly she screamed), but Aunt Kate was different and Susan had a feeling that screaming might be a mistake.

" If you want to stay here you must behave yourself," said Kate firmly, and with that she took up her pen and began to write at a furious pace.

Susan looked at her back. It was a very uncompromising

sort of back, and she was writing about Stephen, of course. Susan hesitated for a few moments and then tip-toed softly out of the room.

It had been touch and go. Kate was fully aware of the fact and was inordinately pleased with the success of her experiment. She waited until the door had closed and then she laid down her pen and heaved a sigh of relief. Susan was amenable to reason ; she was quite sensible. There was nothing wrong with the child, nothing except mismanagement . . . Kate's eyes fell on the piece of paper in front of her. She looked at it in surprise. On it was written a dozen times in her own unmistakable handwriting, *you big stuffed eel*. With a little chuckle of laughter at her own foolishness, Kate tore the paper into very small pieces and dropped it into the waste-paper basket which stood beside her desk.

Susan adored reading ; it was a passion with her ; she read anything that came her way with avid interest. In one way the Dower House suited her well, for it teemed with books, but in another it suited her badly, because Mrs. Dove did not approve of book-worms. Mrs. Dove liked chatting, and in the absence of any one else to chat to she made do with Susan . . . and what is more annoying than to be chatted to when you are absorbed in a book ? Susan needed a hiding-place, that was obvious, and the hiding-place must be chosen with care. She chose the attic. Walter was still working at the shelves, but Walter was a good companion —he liked books too. If you wanted to talk he was quite pleased to indulge in a little conversation, but if he saw you were immersed in a book he left you alone. When she was tired of reading Susan went out and discovered the village. She preferred to explore alone. The village was interesting and the people were friendly ; they all seemed to know who she was. Some of them said " Good morning, Miss Morven," which gave Susan a pleasant feeling of importance, a feeling of belonging somewhere, as she expressed it to herself. She fell into Miss Crease's clutches the first day and was regaled with milk and biscuits and turned inside out, but the experience was unpleasant and Susan took care not to be caught again.

Milly Dove spent a good deal of time hunting for Susan in the house and the garden but so far the attic was inviolate . . . there was a man working in the attic, so she never thought of looking for Susan there. Milly Dove was finding life at the Dower House just a little dull (Kate wrote, Martha was busy, and Susan was no company at all). Having stayed on in the hopes of seeing something of Mr. Morven it was disappointing that he did not come. Why didn't he come, wondered Milly. His daughter was here—one would have thought he would come to see his daughter if for nothing else. Milly suggested this to Kate in what she believed to be a tactful manner, but Kate would not rise. There was some mystery about it, thought Milly, who in some ways was no fool. She missed Minta a good deal, for although they squabbled continually they understood one another and liked the same things ; they spoke the same language, as it were. There was nobody in the Dower House who spoke Milly's language ; nobody who liked a good chat. Milly had to remind herself frequently how comfortable she was in Kate's house and how very much less comfortable she would be all by herself in the London flat ; it was the only way she could bear it. She would go home when Minta returned from Chester, but meantime she really must stay here.

The evenings were not so bad, for Kate did not write in the evening unless Stephen forced her to do so, and, realising that Milly was lonely, Kate set herself out to be entertaining and agreeable to her guest. Sometimes she felt tired after writing all day and would much rather have gone out for a walk or listened peacefully to a little music, but she flattered herself that she could behave like a reasonable being whatever her mood. Kate believed that one had no right to annoy other people by one's moods. Moods were one's own affair and should be dealt with accordingly. She suffered a good deal from those sudden fluctuations of temper which afflict all creative artists, especially when their imagination is at full flood. One day she would be brimming with inexplicable joy and the next plunged in unreasonable gloom. She believed in God, but her faith, instead of burning as a comforting warm fire, would flare up like a flame in the wind or sink into a smouldering heap of ashes. In spite of all this, however, Kate usually managed to be pleasant to her neighbours, and they, taking her at her face value, believed her to be placid and serene.

Milly often annoyed Kate considerably by complaining that *she* was beset by moods and excusing any show of bad temper by saying it was artistic temperament—she arranged flowers so beautifully, of course. "You're *so* lucky," Milly would declare. "You don't know what it is to have *moods*. How I wish I had a nice stodgy nature like you!"

CHAPTER NINETEEN

On Friday morning Kate started to write as usual, but she had come to a troublesome phase in Stephen Slade's adventurous career. It was the point where all the loose ends had to be gathered together and tied into a nice neat bow. Kate felt she needed a breath of fresh air—it also happened that she needed ink and cigarettes—so she decided to run out to the village and obtain all three necessities at the same time.

Miss Crease was in her garden as usual, and as usual she waved and beckoned to Miss Hardy to come and have a chat, but Kate did not dare obey the summons; she was too full of secrets to risk a conversation with Miss Crease.

The village looked extraordinarily peaceful, and Kate, as she walked along, smiled and nodded to several of her friends. She knew a good many people in Old Quinings by this time, and most of them she liked very much indeed. Their attitude to her was curious—they liked her, they were rather proud of her, and they thought her quite crazy. Kate knew this and it amused her . . . she was not above teasing them by pretending to be even more crazy than she really was. It gave the poor souls something to talk about.

Passing Miss Baldwin's, Kate suddenly remembered that Martha wanted tape ; so she stopped, pushed open the door and went in. Miss Baldwin's was one of those amazing shops that sell all manner of " soft goods " from tape and silks to overcoats. Perhaps her chief stand-by was baby linen and children's garments, of which she possessed a varied and attractive assortment.

" Oh, Miss Hardy, " exclaimed Miss Baldwin, " I'm so glad you came in ! (Tape ? Yes, of course . . . white tape ? Yes, certainly). I do hope you were pleased with the little frock, Miss Hardy."

" The little frock ? " said Kate in surprise.

" The pink frock with the white collar and cuffs," explained Miss Baldwin. " I thought little Miss Morven looked *very* sweet in it, the colour suited her so well. I let down the skirt an inch (such long legs she has, hasn't she ?), but otherwise it fitted her a treat. I was so glad I had it in stock. She said just to put it down to your account and you would give me the coupons. I hope that was all right, Miss Hardy."

" Perfectly all right," said Kate.

Kate chuckled as she came out of the shop . . . but it was not really a laughing matter, and she would have to take Susan to task and explain that such things were not done. A *pink* frock, thought Kate, turning the matter over in her mind as she walked back to the Dower House. What did that signify ? Was it just that the wretched child was sick and tired of her pea-green garments or had it a deeper meaning ? Not Lilias, but Susan, thought Kate ; not green, but pink ; not a wanderer upon the face of the earth, but an English child with a line of English forebears.

When Kate got home she heard a murmur of conversation proceeding from the drawing-room, and deciding to have it out with Susan at once, she opened the door and went in. Susan was not there, but Richard was. He and Milly were sitting on the sofa together in earnest conclave.

" Kate, " cried Milly, " I thought you were writing ! "

" We both thought you were writing," declared Richard, rising with a smile. " I was told that the author must on no account be disturbed. Mrs. Dove has been entertaining me."

" I'm glad," said Kate. " I can see you now if you like."

It sounded a little ungracious in Kate's own ears, but Richard did not seem to mind. He followed her into the morning-room and shut the door.

" Such a charming woman," said Richard. " And so absolutely devoted to you, isn't she ? "

" Is she ? " said Kate feebly. " Yes, at least—well, we're sisters, of course."

Richard looked surprised and Kate did not blame him, for obviously he had been listening to eulogisms of Kate and found Kate's response somewhat tepid. She did not blame him for finding Milly attractive—everybody was charmed with Milly at first acquaintance—but all the same she felt just a trifle irritated with Richard.

" She was telling me your plan," continued Richard. " It seems an excellent idea. Of course you can't do anything about it until her daughter is married, but after that event has taken place it will be delightful for you to make a home together."

Kate was almost speechless. " It wouldn't work," she murmured.

" It wouldn't work ? " asked Richard in surprise.

" Milly doesn't like the country and——"

" But she *does* ! " cried Richard. " She's just been telling me how restful she finds it, here in Old Quinings. She has to live in town at present because of Minta, of course. There wouldn't be much here to amuse a young girl——"

" She told you all that ? "

" All that and more. She realises how dull it is for you to live all by yourself. She spoke so warmly of you, so proudly of your success. Her one idea is to be of service to you, to take the housekeeping off your shoulders and leave you free for your work."

Anger and laughter struggled together in Kate's bosom and laughter won. Milly had excelled herself . . . it really was funny. She saw that her hilarity was puzzling Richard, but it was some minutes before she could manage to control it.

"Oh, goodness!" exclaimed Kate at last. "Oh, dear . . . I *am* sorry, but I can't help it. Once I start laughing . . . I can't stop."

"So I see," replied Richard, smiling. "It seems a pity I can't share the joke."

"You didn't come on purpose to see me about that—about Milly's plans for the future, did you, Richard?"

"Good heavens, no, of course not!" he replied. "Perhaps I shouldn't have mentioned the matter. After all, one can't foresee the future—as I said to Mrs. Dove, you might get married."

"What did she say to that?" asked Kate with interest.

"It seemed a new idea to her," Richard admitted. "She said your books were everything to you and that you weren't interested in men."

Kate chuckled. "Well, what *did* you come to see me about, Richard?"

"About my own affairs," he replied, smiling and sitting down. "I went to London for a few days and interviewed my lawyers—that's why I haven't been in to see you before. I hope you missed me, Kate."

"A little."

"Oh, well," said Richard. "A little is better than nothing . . . I spoke to Mr. Weller about a divorce. Wanda is in Switzerland, of course, so nothing much can be done until she returns, but Weller thinks there will be very little difficulty. I don't want to bother you with the sordid details, but the fact that we have not seen one another since 1938 is going to help matters considerably."

"I'm glad," said Kate; and so she was, for having decided that this was the right course, it was good to know that the course would be fairly smooth.

Richard rose and walked to the window and stood there

with his back to the room. " I can't say any more—now,"
said Richard, a trifle huskily.

Kate hesitated. She did not know what to reply. Was
it fair to let Richard think—or hope—that she felt as he
did and that she would marry him when he was free?
And, if it were not fair, how could she tell him that his hopes
had no foundation? She could hardly refuse him until he
proposed, and he could not propose until he was free.
Another man might have done so—but not Richard.
Richard was a delightful person, thought Kate, looking at his
back as he stood at the window. Richard was interesting
and companionable. She liked him immensely. Life with
Richard would be very pleasant indeed ; he was considerate
and kind, they enjoyed the same things. When Kate had
first met Richard she had been drawn to him at once, and
although he was not exactly her " ideal man," she had
vaguely envisaged the possibility that some day if he were
free she might marry him. Kate's ideal of all a man should
be was Stephen, her own creation, but having reached the
age of thirty without finding any one remotely resembling
Stephen, she realised that it was unlikely she ever would.
Richard was not Stephen—but he was a dear. If Richard
had been free and had asked her to marry him a couple
of months ago she would not have refused. Now her
feelings had changed and she knew she could never marry
Richard.

Why can't I ? wondered Kate. Why on earth have I
changed? Is it something in me, or something in Richard?
She thought of Richard's history, the history of his marriage
with Wanda, and there she found the answer to her question.
For Wanda had passed through much the same experience as
herself. Wanda had " fallen for Dickie straight off." Then
her feelings had changed, or cooled off—she " still liked
Dickie quite a lot but not enough to go on living with him
in the Manor for ever and ever, amen." Kate remembered
this ; she understood exactly how Wanda felt, she understood
why Richard had lost Wanda. He was " too soft, too nice,
too civilised " (that's what Wanda had said, and it was true).

Richard *was* too civilised, he was slightly effete, there was too little of the cave-man about him. Richard could inspire love but he could not continue to inspire it . . . he could not keep it alive. She remembered a saying of Martha's; it was something about a man not being a proper man if he could not keep his wife in order. Like most of Martha's sayings it had hit the mark. Kate smiled a little sadly.

"The garden is beginning to look quite nice," said Richard, breaking a long silence.

"Yes, isn't it?" agreed Kate. "I don't know where Abijah gets all the little plants. I wonder . . . he couldn't *steal* them, I suppose."

Richard laughed. He said, "Perhaps he begs or borrows them. I shouldn't worry if I were you, Kate."

They went into the hall and Richard took his hat off the table, "You must come and have tea with me again soon," he said. "Miss Carlyle seems to have deserted me lately. She says she's busy. I suppose you have no idea—I mean she isn't annoyed with me or anything like that?"

"Oh, no, I'm sure it isn't anything like that," said Kate hastily.

"I wanted her to do some typing——" began Richard, and then he stopped suddenly, frozen to a statue, his eyes on the stairs.

Susan was coming downstairs . . . it *was* Susan, but she looked different, Kate noticed. She had combed out her fuzzy bush of hair, parted it in the middle and tied it back with a pink ribbon. She was wearing the pink frock, which suited her remarkably well. Susan was coming down slowly, step by step, as if she were a little doubtful as to her reception.

Kate was about to go forward to meet Susan and reassure her, when she heard Richard draw in his breath in a gasp of astonishment, and turning, saw him leaning against the hall table, his face as white as a sheet.

"Richard, are you ill!" exclaimed Kate.

"It's all right," he replied, pulling himself together with

a visible effort. " I'm perfectly all right. This is—this is Susan, of course."

" Yes, this is Susan," replied Kate, going forward and taking the child's hand.

" I'm your father, Susan," Richard told her.

There was a little pause. It was rather an uncomfortable pause.

" You're very, very good-looking," said Susan, looking up at her father with unconcealed interest and admiration.

They all laughed and the tension was relieved. Afterwards Kate realised how fortunate it was that Susan had said the right thing in the right way (nothing could have been sweeter or more childishly natural), but at the time Kate realised only that Richard had said with absolute conviction, " I'm your father, Susan."

" So you're quite pleased with me?" said Richard, when they had finished laughing. " I'm quite a presentable sort of parent to have. That's lucky, isn't it! I might have been a disappointment, mightn't I? How do you like Old Quinings? I hope you aren't disappointed with it."

" I like it very much, thank you," said Susan politely. " But I want to see the Manor, please."

Richard nodded. " Miss Hardy will bring you to tea."

" And please," said Susan anxiously, " please may I have my own portrait for my very own. It's upstairs in the attic. Walter says is belongs to you."

Richard hesitated. He said, " You found it in the attic, did you? Supposing you go and fetch it for us to see."

" A portrait of Susan——" began Kate when Susan had gone.

" A portrait of Selina Morven," replied Richard. " I don't wonder Susan thought it was herself—the likeness is remarkable. What a queer thing heredity is!" added Richard thoughtfully.

Kate nodded. She had begun to see light.

" The picture is mine, of course," continued Richard, " but Aunt Ellen liked it. She was a strong-minded old lady—a benevolent autocrat; she usually got her own way, so she took the picture and hung it in her dining-room. When Aunt Ellen died the picture disappeared, but I didn't bother about it because I never liked it. Personally I prefer to forget old tragedies—if I can." He walked towards the door.

" You aren't going ? "

" Yes," he replied, smiling a trifly wanly. " Yes, I think so, Kate. I've had about enough for one day. Give Susan my love and tell her she may keep her picture."

" Richard ! " cried Kate, pursuing him onto the door-step. " Richard, wait ! Did you think it was Selina coming downstairs ? "

" Yes. Silly, wasn't it ? " said Richard. He put on his hat and walked away.

CHAPTER TWENTY

SUNDAY was beautiful. It was sunny and warm with blue skies and a light breeze. The Dower House party went to church in the morning (Susan seemed surprised at being taken to church, but on being assured by Aunt Kate that this was the English custom she submitted to the ordeal with a good grace). In the afternoon Milly rested while Kate, accompanied by her recently adopted niece, set forth for a walk on the moor. They chatted in an interesting manner as they went along. Susan had read all the Slade Books now and she assured their author that they were very good indeed.

" There's no silly love business," explained Susan. " I hate love, don't you ? "

Kate was not shocked by this unchristian sentiment ; she knew what Susan meant and was inclined to agree with her— or at least to sympathise. Too much love-interest in novels was apt to be a little cloying.

" You must never let Stephen fall in love," continued

Susan earnestly. "You won't, will you? It would spoil everything. It's quite all right for his friends to fall in love and get married, but not Stephen, ever."

"I shall do all in my power to prevent it," declared Stephen's creator solemnly.

They walked on. The path leading up to the moor wound through a wood. It was a stony track and very steep in parts. Kate was pretty certain that this was the path Abijah had mentioned in his horrible story of Selina Morven. It was the path taken by the devil's disciples on their way to the "stones." Kate was anxious to see the place where Black Mass had been celebrated, but perhaps not to-day. She had a feeling that the place where such wickedness had been perpetrated was a bad place, and might remain unhealthy. She did not want to take Susan there.

"I *do* like you, Aunt Kate," said Susan suddenly. "I'll stay with you always, I think. Wanda doesn't want me—not really—she has lots of people. She has Nat. Some day she's going to marry Nat, you know."

"Is she," said Kate. The news that Wanda had another husband in view was not surprising. Kate had thought it a possibility if not a probability. She hoped "Nat" would be able to keep Wanda in order; she hoped he was not "too soft, too nice, too civilised." She wondered if Wanda would let her keep Susan. Kate was busy with her thoughts and was considerably startled by Susan's next remark.

"'All women labouring of child!'" said Susan, quoting from the Litany which had been read in church that morning. "That's you, of course, isn't it?"

"Me!" exclaimed Kate, with a gasp of astonishment. "No, certainly not."

"It is *in a way*," argued Susan. "Of course I know that it really means nurses who have to look after little children and get paid for their work, but you're looking after me, Aunt Kate."

"It's a labour of love," declared Aunt Kate, and, so saying, she sat down upon a conveniently placed boulder and laughed until she cried.

"I suppose it doesn't mean that at all," said Susan, watching her unsmilingly.

The moor was a delightful place to walk. It rolled away westwards to a ridge of hills and was dotted with clumps of trees and seamed with watercourses. There were thousands of tiny wild-flowers and patches of heather not yet in bloom. Here and there an outcrop of rock had broken through the thin skin of earth. Susan was charmed with the moor; she ran about in delight, she picked flowers and dabbled her hands in the little streams. Kate sat down with her back against a rock and watched her enjoying herself.

It was warm and sunny. A scent of thyme filled the air. The only sounds were the trickle of the stream and the hum of bees. Kate was almost asleep when suddenly she heard a different sound, and, opening her eyes, saw Walter Stack standing some yards away and looking at her.

"Walter!" exclaimed Kate. "What are you doing here?"

"I intended to fish," he replied, pointing to his rod and creel, "but the sun is far too bright. It's not worth trying." He sat down beside her as he spoke.

Kate knew nothing of fishing so she made no comment, for she did not want to betray her ignorance of the ways and habits of fish.

"I often come up here," continued Walter. "It's soothing. I don't really mind if I catch any fish or not. Susan is enjoying herself, isn't she?"

"We're all enjoying ourselves," replied Kate. "I was nearly asleep. I thought at first I was dreaming when I saw you standing there."

"I wonder why?" said Walter.

"Perhaps because I dreamt about you the other night," said Kate thoughtfully. "It was a curious dream. I've been wondering what it meant—if dreams mean anything."

Walter smiled. He said, "'Oh, King, live for ever; tell thy servant thy dream and he will show the interpretation.'"

Kate hesitated for a moment. She had not really intended to tell Walter but it seemed silly to refuse. She told him about the fair, broad estuary and the little ship and the three men who had been her companions on the voyage. When she had finished there was silence.

"Well?" said Kate, smiling. "You know what happened to the Chaldeans who could not interpret Nebuchadnezzar's dream."

"I was in good company, wasn't I?" said Walter in a thoughtful voice.

"Tell on," said Kate. "What was the interpretation thereof?"

"The interpretation is beyond me, but I know what caused the dream," said Walter slowly. "You admire courage, don't you? I wonder why you place it so high amongst the attributes of man."

"Because it's the basis of everything. A man without courage is only half a man—and to be honest, the same applies to a woman."

"Drake is the personification of courage," continued Walter thoughtfully. "He was England's hero, he has been her inspiration for centuries. Stephen is your own creation, your own idea of what a man should be. As for Walter Stack," said Walter, looking at her and smiling, "I'm afraid he was there by reason of his D.S.O. An insufficient reason to admit him to the company of giants, I assure you. It was a tame performance compared with the adventures of his companions."

"People aren't decorated for tame deeds," replied Kate, smiling in return.

There was a short silence while Kate considered the interpretation of her dream. It was good as far as it went but it did not go far enough. Walter had not interpreted the melting of the three figures into one, and to Kate that had seemed the most important part. She remembered it clearly. The three men had been distinct and separate and then their outlines had become a trifle blurred . . . and then they had become one . . . one solitary figure standing at the bows of the ship. Kate opened her mouth to explain this to Walter and to ask what it meant, and then she paused, for she had seen the meaning herself. It was perfectly clear and perfectly simple . . . and absolutely astounding. England's hero and the hero of her own creation were fused in the hero of to-day . . . he was Walter.

Kate gasped ; she was overwhelmed by the magnitude of her discovery.

" It really was tame," declared Walter. He was sitting with his hands round his knees, gazing at the sunlit moor. " I blew up a bridge, that's all. We were retreating, you see, and the bridge had to be blown up after we had crossed. It wasn't much of a bridge, but it spanned a deep ravine which would delay the Japs and bother them a good deal —especially their transport. Any one could have done it ; the engineers who mined it wanted to stay and finish the job, but engineers were scarce—they weren't expendable. I was obviously the fellow to stay behind and send the bridge sky-high. It was rather fun, really, especially as the bridge was chock-a-block with little yellow devils when I pressed the button . . . it seems strange to think of it *here* and *now*," added Walter in a low voice as he looked round the peaceful scene.

Kate could well believe it and was about to say so, but their conversation was interrupted by Susan, who had got tired of splashing in the stream, and, climbing onto the rocks behind them, had been listening with interest to Walter's tale.

" Did it go up with a noise like thunder ? " she inquired.

Walter laughed and assured her that the noise had been most satisfactory.

" And Walter," said Susan, as she slid down the rock, " Walter, tell me. Were there bits of little yellow devils flying about in the air ? "

Walter hesitated. " I didn't notice," he said uncomfortably.

" Aw, come on, Walter, spill the beans," implored Susan.

" I've spilt enough for one afternoon," declared Walter with a grin.

The three of them walked home together. Susan, with her hand in Walter's, hopped and skipped along and talked without ceasing ; (Kate had never seen her so childishly natural before). She told him that the portrait of herself was now her very own and asked if he would come and hang it for her in her bedroom.

" I'm going to stay with Aunt Kate always," declared Susan. " I'm an English girl, you see. I'm going to an English school and I'm going to wear all different coloured clothes—all except green. You like my pink frock, don't you, Walter ? When it's worn out I think I shall have a blue one. Aunt Kate will buy it for me out of the money she makes writing books . . . Well, she hasn't actually said so, but I expect it will be all right. Walter, do you like me best with my hair all fuzzy or straight like it is in my picture ? I like it straight best, but it won't stay straight for more than ten minutes. I wonder how the man who painted my portrait knew what I looked like with my hair straight. I wonder how he knew what I looked like *at all* . . . it *is* funny, isn't it, Walter ? "

Kate was glad of Susan's chatter. It seemed ridiculous to feel shy of Walter, but her recent discovery had shaken her a good deal and she wanted time and quiet thought to adjust herself. All women have the picture of an ideal man in their hearts, and Kate was no exception to the rule. Hitherto she had met nobody who approached that ideal —except Stephen, of course. Kate had created Stephen and endowed him with all the attributes she admired : courage, modesty, humour, kindliness, and a stubborn sense of duty, a stubborn determination to stand by his principles through thick and thin. She realised that she had done this, she realised that Stephen was her ideal man, and she had decided that she would never find a man of flesh and blood to measure up to the standard she had set. Now she had found him.

Kate glanced at him several times as they went down the steep path together (with Susan between them chattering like a little magpie). She saw him smiling down at Susan, teasing her, entering into her fun. She thought of his courage in the war, and the different sort of courage with which he was tackling his own private battle ; she thought of the modest way he had of belittling his achievements. But all this was nothing in comparison with the amazing discovery that she loved Walter. How blind she had been not to discover this before ! How stupid not to realise why she had always been so interested in him, so delighted when he came to the house, so happy and comfortable when she knew he was under her roof . . . I've always loved him, thought Kate, glancing at him again and feeling her heart go out to him in a flood of tenderness. I loved him long before I knew him. He's Stephen, of course.

Was there any chance that her feeling for Walter was returned ? Very little, really, decided Kate, who was nothing if not honest with herself. She knew he liked her and valued her friendship, but that was not love . . . he had never said one word nor looked one look which showed more than friendship.

" And what does Aunt Kate think about all this ? " inquired Walter, smiling at her over Susan's head.

" Aunt Kate " had not heard a word of " all this," of course, but she did her best to smile back in a friendly manner. " Susan is a little chatterbox," she said.

Walter had enjoyed his Sunday afternoon on the moor ; he had caught no fish but he felt soothed and rested. He walked up the little path to the Lodge Cottage, and, going through to the kitchen, discovered his mother sitting at the table writing a letter. Mrs. Stack wrote a good letter, a letter which expressed her personality—as Walter had cause to know—but the composition took time and immense concentration. She was not a ready writer.

Mrs. Stack looked up when Walter came in and slid her

letter beneath the blotting-paper. " Did you have a nice afternoon ? " she inquired.

" Very nice," replied Walter, smiling down at her. " I suppose you've spent the afternoon writing to Bertie, haven't you ? "

" Oh, Walter, I wasn't going to bother you ! How *did* you guess ? "

" Your guilty looks betrayed you. How much has he asked you for ? "

" Don't you worry," replied Mrs. Stack. " You've plenty to worry about without worrying about Bertie."

" But, Mother, I can easily——"

" Now, Walter," interrupted Mrs. Stack, looking up at him over the top of her spectacles. " Now, Walter, we'll just have this straight. I won't have you starting sending money to Bertie. It's got nothing to do with you."

Walter looked thoughtful. " I think I'll go and see Bertie," he said. " I'll see if I can't get him into a decent job. Perhaps I could put him on his feet."

" You couldn't," declared Mrs. Stack. " It wouldn't be a bit of use. I've put Bertie on his feet half a dozen times. He won't stand on them, that's what's the matter with *him*. The more you do for Bertie the less he does for himself. No, Walter, you're a lot cleverer than me in some ways, but you don't understand Bertie. You'll do as I say in this."

" Say on, then, Mrs. Solomon," said Walter, trying to raise a smile.

Mrs. Stack smiled rather half-heartedly. " You and your jokes ! " she said. " But I *will* say on, because I know what I'm talking about. It's like this, Walter. If Bertie wants money very badly he writes to me because he knows I couldn't let him starve. He knows I can't spare very much—though to be honest with you he's had money I could ill afford to send. Well, that's all right. He knows pretty well how much he can get out of me, but if you start sending money you'll never get leave to stop."

Walter stood for a few moments gazing out of the window. "You *are* Mrs. Solomon," he said.

"Well, just you do as I say, Walter," said "Mrs. Solomon," smiling at him affectionately. "You're to have nothing at all to do with Bertie, and if you get a letter from him you're to hand it over to me."

Walter laughed. He took a letter out of his pocket and handed it to her.

"There!" exclaimed Mrs. Stack. "There now! Trying to get money out of both of us at the same time—that's Bertie all over. Now, Walter, you're not to send him a penny. Promise me, Walter."

"I promise," replied Walter, laughing. "You know quite well I always do what you tell me."

Part Three

CHAPTER TWENTY-ONE

MONDAY was pay day for Abijah. He preferred it that way
for some obscure reason of his own, and it was all one to
Kate. She might have forgotten to pay him, but Abijah
took care of that ; he made a point of obtruding himself
upon his employer's notice every Monday morning. To-day
he was hoeing the path just outside the morning-room
windows, so his employer not only saw him but heard him
as well.

It was marvellous how he was getting the place cleared
up ; and Kate, feeling slightly less repugnance than usual
for her tame gnome, went out to pay him his due and
conversed with him pleasantly for a few minutes.

" I've sacked that boy," said Abijah, stowing his money
away securely in an inner pocket. " Lazy, that's what 'e
wor—bone idle. No good to me, 'e worn't."

" Can you get someone else ? " inquired Kate.

" We doan't need nobody," he replied. " Lily's 'ere this
marnin'. Good little worker, Lily is ; worth 'alf a dozen
lazy boys."

" Shouldn't she be at school ? "

" School ! " exclaimed Abijah in disgust. " School ain't
no use to Lily. They doan't larn 'er nothin' useful. Prickin'
out seedlin's is useful work."

" You'll get into trouble if you keep her away from
school."

" I bin in trouble afore, that doan't worry me," Abijah
replied, and he spat contemptuously onto the path.

Kate's repugnance returned in full measure.

" Wot right 'ave they to make Lily go to school ? "
continued Abijah, working himself up into a rage. " Lily
doan't like school, she never 'as liked school. There's them

that likes school an' them that doan't. Lily ain't goin'
back, never, not if I knows it."

"But, Abijah——"

"They can send me to prison," declared Abijah angrily.
"If that's wot they want let 'em come an' take me. They
woan't get Lily, not if I knows it. Narsty to Lily, that's
wot they are—narsty as can be. Lily ain't going back, never;
she doan't need no more book-larnin'."

"She *does* need it," asserted Kate. "It isn't fair to Lily
to keep her away from school. It's dreadful for a girl of
her age not to be able to read or write."

"'Oo says Lily carn't read or write!" cried Abijah, and
with that he seized his hoe and attacked the weeds in a fury.

Kate watched him for a few moments. She would have
liked to pursue the conversation (it had interesting possi-
bilities), but obviously Abijah was in no mood for further
dalliance. She left him hoeing as if his life depended upon
it and went into the house.

Somehow or other Kate could not get this conversation
out of her mind. It pestered her; she thought about it off
and on all day. "Who says Lily can't read or write?"
Well, Anne Carlyle had said so and she ought to know,
but her standard of "book-larnin'" was probably a good
deal higher than Abijah's. According to Abijah, Lily had
absorbed all the education she needed, so she must have
learnt a little in spite of Anne Carlyle's assertion to the
contrary. . . . "A little learning is a dangerous thing," said
a voice in Kate's brain. She smiled to herself at this new
application of the old saying, but it was a thoughtful smile,
for it had just struck Kate that in Lily's case a little learning
might be very dangerous indeed. If Lily could write—a
little—she and Abijah together fulfilled all the requirements
of the poison pen. Abijah with his sly propensities could
easily have obtained the necessary information, and his
gnome-like nature would prompt him to make mischief in
this underhand way. Lily with her "little learning" could
easily have written the messages which had caused so much
vexation.

Kate brooded over the matter until she could bear it no longer. She decided to put her suspicions to the test.

Lily was working in the potting-shed; she was pricking out seedlings and was so absorbed in her task that she did not hear Kate's approach, so Kate was able to stand and watch her for a few moments unperceived. Kate had not seen Lily before, but had heard a good deal about her and was interested to behold her in the flesh. She had expected Abijah's granddaughter to resemble him; but no, she did not resemble him in the least. Lily was a well-made girl, tall and strong; she was remarkably neat and clean considering her upbringing, thought Kate in surprised approval.

Lily was enjoying her task and doing it extremely well; neatly, quickly, lovingly Lily's fingers separated the tiny plants and tucked them into the soil. There was something about Lily that touched Kate's heart; she decided that the girl must be given a chance to make good. It would not be difficult to help her, for she was a born gardener. But first everything must be cleared up, not only for the sake of other people, but for Lily's own sake.

" Lily," said Kate, pushing the door open, " Lily, I *do* think it was silly of you to give Tommy Rogers a shilling for writing that letter to Mrs. Morven."

" I never did ! " cried Lily, turning in sudden alarm. " 'Oo said I did ! There worn't no need to give nobody nothin'. I wrote it myself——"

" You could be sent to prison for that, you know," interrupted Kate. " I don't know if you could be sent to prison for frightening little children and teaching them to play at witches, but——"

" Lor', 'ow d'you know about that ! " exclaimed Lily in horrified tones.

Kate restrained the impulse to tell Lily that nothing was hid from her—chiefly because it might seem to Lily that further questions would be unnecessary.

" I didden' do nothin'," cried Lily, who during the little pause had regained her scattered wits and realised her

danger. " You ain't got no right to come over me an' say
things that ain't true. I didden' do nothin' wrong. It wor
a game, that's all. The spell wor a game, too—it wor all
a game—it didden' do Tommy no 'arm."

Kate saw that this would take time and patience, but
as Lily could not escape there was no hurry about it; none
at all. Kate leant against the side of the door and lighted
a cigarette. She was determined to get to the bottom of the
matter, to turn Lily inside out, and she had no scruples
whatever in using all the means in her power—short of
torture. It was lucky that she had profited so much from
her little chats with Miss Crease, thought Kate.

Having decided upon her plan of action, Kate set to
work in earnest and proceeded to catechise her prisoner
thoroughly and mercilessly. She employed all the methods
Miss Crease had taught her, and even invented one of her
own to extort a piece of information which Lily seemed
particularly reluctant to disclose.

" Tell me," said Kate, taking half a crown out of her
pocket and looking at it thoughtfully, " tell me *truthfully*
who wrote the address on the envelope of the letter you
sent to Mrs. Morven in America."

" The girl in the post office," said Lily, eyeing the
silver coin.

" What did you tell the girl ? "

" I told 'er Mrs. Morven 'ad sent me stockin's an' I
wor writin' to thank 'er. Granfer told me to. Granfer said
the girl would know Mrs. Morven's address—an' so she
did."

The coin changed hands.

By this time Lily was completely bamboozled. Miss
Hardy seemed to know everything, and she jumped about
from one thing to another in the most confusing way. Lily
tried to twist and turn. She contradicted herself flatly half
a dozen times ; she lied when she could, but her lies did
no good at all, for Miss Hardy seemed to know when she
was lying and to guess the truth. And all the time Miss
Hardy leant against the door of the potting-shed and smoked

and remained perfectly calm . . . almost friendly, thought
Lily, hunting about desperately for a way of escape.

"Come now, Lily," Miss Hardy said, "you've told
me this before, so it's no use going back on it now. That
would be silly, wouldn't it? You wrote that letter to Miss
Carlyle and you put it in her desk."

"In 'er waterproof pocket," declared Lily, taken
unawares.

"A much better place," said Miss Hardy, nodding
cheerfully. "And the letter you wrote to Mr. Morven—
you gave that to Mrs. Haygarth, didn't you?"

"No, I never," declared Lily. "There worn't no need.
I jus' slipped it in the letter-box, but I never wrote no
letter to Mr. Morven! I never said I did."

"You slipped it into the letter-box, of course," said
Miss Hardy, nodding.

"I tell you I never wrote no letter to Mr. Morven."

"But you've just told me you slipped it into the letter-
box," Miss Hardy pointed out. "You couldn't have
slipped it into the letter-box unless you had written it, you
know. Now tell me about the spell."

"I don't know nothin' about no spell."

"Did you make the spell all by yourself, Lily?"

"It didden' do Tommy no 'arm."

"That was because you didn't know how to do it, of
course."

"I did, then," asserted Lily defiantly. "A proper
mommet, it wor."

"Who helped you to make it?" asked Miss Hardy
with interest.

So it went on. It was most reprehensible, of course,
bribery combined with brow-beating and third degree.
Kate had no right whatever to take the law into her own
hands and extort a confession from her prisoner. But surely
it was better, thought Kate, silencing her doubts as to the
morality of the proceeding, surely it was better to clear up
the whole thing and give the girl a chance than to hand
her over to the police to deal with.

CHAPTER TWENTY-TWO

ANNE CARLYLE called at the Dower House after the nine
o'clock news and found Kate sitting at her desk, writing.

" Sit down and take a cigarette," said Kate. " I won't
be a minute."

Anne took a cigarette and sat down. She looked at the
author enviously. How delightful it would be if one could
write like that—so easily and at such a furious pace. If one
could write there would be no need to teach a crowd of
semi-idiotic children to read and write and add. As a rule
Anne liked her work immensely, but she was depressed and
worried ; she was even rather frightened, for unless she got
to the bottom of the mystery soon she might find herself in
serious trouble—she might lose her job. It was a shame to
bother Miss Hardy—Kate—with her problems, but she had
to have someone in whom to confide and there was nobody
else in Old Quinings, nobody who would understand,
nobody whom she could trust. She could trust Kate (Kate
had a wonderfully rock-like stability). At first she had
thought Kate rather a plain woman, but now that she
knew her she was amazed at her own unperspicacity. Kate
was much more than good-looking : her face was so
interesting, so alive, so vital. What a splendid couple they
would make, she and Mr. Morven ! thought Anne with
a little sigh.

" There," said Kate, collecting her papers and clipping
them together. " That's finished. That's the whole story
of the witch with the poison pen."

Anne stared at her in dumb amazement.

" Yes," said Kate, laughing. " Yes, I've solved the
mysteries—the two mysteries are really one—and I've
written it all down."

" You've written it all down ! "

Kate looked a trifle self-conscious. " It was such a

muddle," she explained. " I got it piecemeal from the wretched girl and I wanted to get it straight. My experience is that if you want to get a thing straightened out the best way is to write it down ; besides," added Kate with a deprecating smile, " besides, it's so intensely interesting. It's a human document, a fascinating study in psychology. Of course I can't use it—ever—but I shall certainly keep it for my own delectation."

" May I see it ? " asked Anne, who at the moment was more concerned with the solution of her personal problems than with Kate's ideas about psychology.

Kate hesitated and then handed it over with a reluctant air. " It's terribly rough," she said. " I haven't read it over. You may not be able to read my writing."

Anne took the papers without comment. Another woman, less reasonable, might have asked for verbal information and inquired how the problems had been solved and who was the villain of the piece. Anne was eminently reasonable. She put on a pair of tortoiseshell spectacles and began to read.

" Lily Rannish lived with her grandfather in a small cottage on the Morven estate. She had lived there as long as she could remember. Her grandfather, Abijah, told her that both her parents were dead. Abijah was fond of Lily and very kind to her according to his lights. Sometimes he talked a lot and told her stories of the old days, stories which his grandfather had told him ; but at other times he was completely silent and did not speak to her for days on end. In spite of this lonely existence Lily was happy and contented, for she had plenty to do and she liked keeping the little house in order. What she enjoyed most, however, was wandering about the moor, finding little plants and bringing them home and planting them in the garden.

" The days passed very pleasantly until Lily was dis-covered by the school authorities and her grandfather was informed that the child must attend school. Abijah was furious ; he had had no education himself and he did not hold with book-learning ; besides, he needed his grand-

daughter at home. Lily was reluctant to be educated ;
books had no charm for her ; but in spite of the protests of
Abijah and his granddaughter Lily was obliged to go to
school. She went as seldom as possible and she learnt as
little as she could. This was her way of showing her disap-
proval of the system of compulsory education, of proclaiming
to herself—and perhaps to others—that she was a free
agent and not a slave . . ."

Anne looked up and said, " This sounds more like Kate
Hardy than Lily Rannish. What does Lily know of compulsory education ? "

" More than most people," retorted Kate. " Lily has
sampled it and disapproves."

" Surely Kate Hardy doesn't disapprove of it ? "
exclaimed Anne in horrified tones.

" I hate compulsion in any form," declared Kate. " I
realise children should be educated, but need they be
dragged into it by brute force ? Isn't there some other
way ? Couldn't they be taught the subjects they like ? "

" To the exclusion of other subjects ! "

" Surely there's some way of doing it."

Anne could think of none. She was a little displeased
with Kate. She picked up the manuscript and continued
to read.

" The only lesson Lily enjoyed was botany. She was
interested in flowers and plants of all kinds ; she often
found rare specimens on the moor and took them to school.
Miss Carlyle told her their names and their habits. If
lessons had consisted entirely of nature-studies Lily would
not have minded going to school, but unfortunately they
did not. Lily deliberately shut her mind to other lessons ;
she found it was possible to do so by thinking of something
else ; it was difficult at first, but as time went on it became
easier—it became a habit.

" About six months ago Abijah asked Lily if she could
write a letter for him. She tore a piece of paper out
of a school exercise book and together they composed it.
Abijah was surprised to find that his granddaughter was

able to write a letter ; he was not only surprised but pleased. There was something in this school business after all—not much, perhaps, but a little. Lily was a clever girl. After that Lily wrote another letter for Abijah, she found the task to her taste.

"Soon after the episode of the first anonymous letter Lily suddenly 'grew up'—this was her own expression, and I feel it describes the change in her psychological condition quite clearly—she grew up and became conscious of herself and other people, became unsatisfied with her lot, began to look at the world with a new and different vision, began to think about the future. What was Lily's future ? Did she intend to live with her grandfather for ever ? No ; some day she would get married like other girls . . . but would she ? That was the question. Her school-fellows despised her, they laughed at her because she was a dunce, because she was dirty and ragged and uncouth. This had not mattered before when she was sufficient unto herself, but now it mattered a good deal. She decided to take more care of her personal appearance. Miss Carlyle noticed that Lily had mended her clothes and looked cleaner and more tidy. But Miss Carlyle was the only person who cared ; her school-fellows were just as scornful and unfriendly. Lily became more and more unhappy ; she wanted people to like her, but, failing that, she wanted to show them that she was not to be despised. She wanted power. This desire upon Lily's part was the beginning of all the trouble . . . the desire for power. If people did not like her they must be made to respect her, perhaps even to fear her.

"Lily began her campaign by teaching some of the younger children to play at scatterers, and to make the game more interesting she told them stories about the people they were intended to represent. The stories scared them considerably but they came back for more. Lily had a large repertory of hair-raising stories which she had heard from her grandfather. She retailed them with advantages, and her fame as a story-teller spread rapidly round the school. Many of the older children, who had ignored and scorned her, changed their attitude completely and joined her little group. In a few weeks' time the children knew a great deal about the bad old days, about witches and warlocks who had pursued their baleful activities in the neighbourhood of Old Quinings and suffered for their sins. They had heard about witches' covens which had taken place on the moor, not a mile from their homes; they had heard about different kinds of magic; how one witch would make a waxen image of the person she wanted to harm and would transfix it with pins or melt it in a flame; how another would gather herbs and brew potions; and still another would ill-wish her victim and blast him with the power of the evil eye. They listened with bated breath to the list of disorders which afflicted those who were unfortunate enough to incur the displeasure of a witch, ' their colour fadeth, their flesh rotteth, their speech is benumbed and their senses are bereft.'

" The children were sworn to secrecy (that was part of the ' game '), but some of them talked in their sleep and their parents spoke to Miss Carlyle about it. Miss Carlyle began to suspect that something was going on, and Lily decided that she must be removed. Having learnt the trick of anonymous letters, Lily composed one for Miss Carlyle and put it into the pocket of her waterproof, which hung in the children's cloakroom."

Anne looked up and said, " How on earth did you manage to get all this out of Lily Rannish ? She's practically speechless in school."

" I squeezed her," admitted Kate.

" But there's a great deal here that Lily couldn't have told you, however hard you squeezed."

Kate nodded. " I knew a little before and suspected a good deal. Perhaps I imagined some of it, but I had a good solid foundation for my imagination to build on. I think you may take the document as true."

" It sounds true," said Anne, looking at the author with increased respect.

The document continued : " There were several children

in school who refused to have anything to do with Lily, and amongst these was Tommy Rogers. He was the greatest stumbling-block in Lily's path. Lily disliked Tommy intensely, for he was everything that she was not, everything that in her heart of hearts she wanted to be. Tommy was clever, he was a favourite with Miss Carlyle and popular with his contemporaries, he was clean and tidy and always neatly dressed, he had a good home and kind parents, he had sisters and brothers as well. It seemed unfair that Tommy should have so much and Lily so little, nothing at all except the power which she had won for herself—and this power, which had seemed so desirable, was now beginning to prove a little irksome. The children had begun to fear Lily. The idea grew that Lily herself was a witch."

Anne Carlyle put down the manuscript and said, " This is a frightful story ! "

" But interesting, isn't it ? " said the author, perhaps a trifle smugly, for to tell the truth it had been a most enthralling story to write : it was so penetrating in its exposure of the quirks of human nature, it was so simple and yet so dramatic. It was Life.

" The idea that Lily was a witch was at first confined to the younger children. They whispered about it amongst themselves, they frightened themselves and one another with little stories, silly little stories concerning Lily's activities at night. She knew about herbs, of course ; she had been seen gathering them at night by the light of the full moon : nightshade, hellebore, foxgloves and precious bane. Someone had seen a hare ; it had sat up and looked round, it had peered over its shoulder at the terrified beholder—just like Lily—and then, quite suddenly, it had disappeared. Lily began to get a little frightened of her own reputation ; she began to think it was time to stop. But when one has gone too far down the hill, and too fast, it is difficult to stop. Besides, she had two faithful followers who were still enthusiastic about the game. They urged her on, they encouraged her, they besought her to try her hand at a real spell.

"On Thursday afternoon after the other children had gone home, Lily and her two satellites made an image of Tommy Rogers. They made it of candle-grease, which is not an easy medium, and it took them some time to complete their task. The ' mommet ' was not very like Tommy, but fortunately Lily had managed to obtain a few of Tommy's hairs—these were incorporated in the ' mommet ' —so there was no doubt as to whom it was intended to represent. The three conspirators had begun to make their spell in dead earnest. They had fully intended to complete Tommy's discomfiture by transfixing his image with a pin, but when they saw the completed image lying upon Lily's desk, ready for the next stage, the last and most important stage in their experiment, their hearts misgave them. They were a little frightened. They assured one another that it was just a game, it could do Tommy no harm (how could it do Tommy any harm ?) but in spite of these assurances there was an odd sort of tension in the air, an unpleasant kind of excitement. ' You do it, Lily,' said the satellites with one voice, but Lily was reluctant. Lily hesitated. She was still hesitating, pin in hand, when Miss Carlyle came into the schoolroom. There was only one thing to be done : they raised the lid of Lily's desk and slipped the image inside.

" Lily could not sleep that night ; she tossed and turned restlessly. Why had she consented to try the spell ? Why had she left the thing in her desk ? Miss Carlyle might find it and guess what it was. Somebody else might find it. Towards morning Lily dropped into a very uneasy sleep and dreamt confusedly. All the stories which Abijah had told her and which she had passed on to the other children were jumbled up together in Lily's dream, and Lily herself was there in the midst of the horrors. It was night and the moon was shining, Old Quinings seemed different to Lily in her dream. The people were different too ; they were fierce and noisy, they looked at her with scowling faces and smouldering eyes . . . they pushed her roughly and tore her clothes ; they dragged her to the village-green. There Lily saw a huge bonfire blazing, with flames shooting up like red and yellow tongues and black smoke towering into the air. Lily struggled and fought with her captors, ' No ! ' she cried in agonised tones. ' No, I'm not a witch ! It was just a game ! ' She was still shouting at the top of her voice when she awoke.

" She was so upset and frightened and miserable that she did not want to go to school, but she had to go, because the image was in her desk. She decided to go to school early, before the other children arrived, to get the image and destroy it. When Lily opened her desk she discovered that the wax had melted and the head of the image had fallen off . . ."

The manuscript slipped from Anne's hands and fell with a rustle on to the floor. " Tommy is ill ! " she exclaimed.

Kate laughed. She could not help it.

" He's ill," repeated Anne, looking at her with eyes like saucers.

" Don't tell me that he's lost his head ! "

" He's got pains in his head and a temperature," declared Anne. " He has been in bed since Friday morning."

" Really, Anne ! " cried Kate, trying to control her mirth. " Really, you are a little goose ! You've been over-working Tommy, of course, stuffing his poor little head to bursting point—no wonder it aches ! "

Anne drew her hand across her eyes and smiled uncertainly. " It was silly of me," she agreed. " It's your fault for making it so horribly real . . . but even if I don't believe in Lily's spell, other people will."

" Other people mustn't know. Who's going to tell them ? Not you nor I, and certainly not Lily nor either of her accomplices. The whole thing is over and finished with. You ought to be jumping with joy."

" Of course I'm glad—and very, very grateful."

" That's better," nodded Kate. " That's the spirit, Anne. All you've got to do now is to go home and find the 'mommet,' which, incidentally, is still concealed in Lily's desk. Lily was too shaken by her discovery to remove it from its hiding-place."

"What shall I do with it?" asked Anne.

"That's for you to decide," declared Kate with a serious air. "I can't tell you the right procedure, I'm afraid. It might be rather risky to destroy it. Perhaps you had better stick on Tommy's head, wrap him carefully in cotton-wool and put him in a glass case. How would that do?"

"You are a wretch," said Anne, smiling.

"I'll tell you what to do," said Kate, struck by a brilliant notion. "Your best plan will be to go and ask Richard Morven to lend you a book on witchcraft."

They both laughed.

"I can—now, can't I?" said Anne quite cheerfully.

"You must," replied Kate. "Richard would be hurt if you stopped going to the Manor. He told me the other day that you seemed to be very busy just now. Do go, Anne. He likes you to make use of his books."

"I will," said Anne, nodding.

"As for Lily," continued Kate, "Lily must go away. She must be given a chance to make good. I'm determined on that; the wretched girl has never had a chance. Fortunately I happen to know a man who runs a market-garden. I used to get my vegetables from him when we lived in town. He'll be delighted to have a girl with green fingers; the fact that she is a reformed witch won't worry him in the least."

"I hope she is reformed," said Anne, laughing quite naturally.

"She's had a severe lesson," nodded Kate.

Anne rose to go. She said, "You know, Kate, you remind me a little of old Miss Morven. She used to enjoy arranging other people's affairs."

"The Dower House air breeds benevolent autocrats," replied Kate, who, oddly enough, had been thinking the same thing herself.

CHAPTER TWENTY-THREE

Mr. Seager was worried. He was also very angry. The whole thing seemed perfectly clear to him and perfectly fair. Here was Walter Stack, back from the War, having fought for his country and won the D.S.O. into the bargain. Mr. Seager had given him back his old job as he had promised to do; everything was straight and above-board. Mr. Seager was obliged by law to take Stack back, so he had no option in the matter; but the promise counted with Mr. Seager every bit as much as any law made by Parliament—he was that sort of man. Mr. Seager had explained all this to his other workmen not once but several times. He had explained it clearly and patiently, although no explanation should have been necessary, for the men had known all along that Stack was coming back. Reuben Doubleday had been Stack's special friend and had stepped into Stack's shoes on the distinct understanding that he was filling them temporarily; and the others—Turner, Curtis and Robinson—knew it too. It wasn't as if they were getting less pay, either; they were getting exactly the same, yet in spite of this they were discontented. They grumbled and growled and talked amongst themselves and scamped their work. (Mr. Seager would have liked to sack the lot, but how could he? Where would he get other men to fill their places?) And that wasn't the worst of the business; the worst was they were giving Stack a hell of a time. Stack was looking wretched. If only Stack would go, thought Seager. The man was an excellent workman and could easily find work elsewhere . . . but Seager wasn't going to advise Stack to leave Old Quinings, because—well, because it wasn't fair. If Stack wanted to stay here he had every right to stay. Seager had given his promise seven years ago and he intended to keep it . . . Bob Seager was almost as stubborn as Walter Stack.

Seager could do a good deal to lighten Stack's lot and he did all he could. He arranged the work so that Stack got individual jobs where he could work alone; the Dower House jobs for instance. Miss Hardy was delighted with the work he had done for her, and no wonder—Stack had made a fine job of those shelves. Now Miss Hardy wanted the old barn put in order and it was high time, too. There was a lot of junk in the rafters, and all that would have to be cleared before the rafters could be properly examined and repaired.

" Take the long ladder," said Seager. " It's high, that barn is. I'll come and have a look at the rafters when you've got them cleared of rubbish."

Stack had to carry the ladder from Seager's workshop to the barn. It would have been natural to send two men with the ladder, but Seager hesitated to give the order, and while he was hesitating Stack shouldered it and walked away. He was strong, thought Seager, watching him as he walked off with the long ladder balanced on his shoulder. Seager tipped his cap forward and scratched his head—a problem, that's what it was.

The other men had been detailed for other work : two to mend some fencing on the Morven property and two to go up to Miss Crease. She had been pestering Seager for weeks to send her a couple of men to look at her roof. The men stood in Seager's yard and talked. Doubleday laughed and gestured with his thumb at Stack's receding figure.

Seager was annoyed. He was annoyed not only because it was his time they were wasting but because they were discussing Stack, making fun of him. He came out of his office and said, " Supposing you stop talking and do a bit of work ! "

" Like Stack," said Doubleday impudently.

The others sniggered.

" You'll never be as good a man as Stack, that's certain," declared Seager.

" My work's as good as his any day and you know it ! " exclaimed Doubleday in furious tones.

"I'm not talking about your work," returned Seager significantly.

Meantime Walter Stack had reached the barn. He was hot but not tired, for he was of tremendously strong physique and in excellent condition. The day was close and overcast. It was cloudy and there was no wind. Looking over the tree-tops from the slight eminence upon which the barn stood, Walter saw it was dark and raining in the Wandlebury direction, but towards the west there were gaps in the cloud through which the sun was pouring in a silver flood. The country which lay beneath the curtain of cloud had a curiously unreal appearance : everything was unnaturally clear. It was beautiful, Walter thought—the soft clouds and the silvery light and the green country—it was more beautiful than sunshine and blue skies. It was this sort of weather he had pined for when he was sweltering under the brassy glare of the tropical sun. Old Quinings ! He loved the place. Would he be able to stay ?

Walter had made very little headway with the other men. They still resented him. Turner was the only one who had shown the slightest signs of thawing. Turner was not a bad fellow—a bit weak, of course, and too much under the influence of Reuben Doubleday, but Walter had managed to get him alone last night and they had had a drink together at the Bull and Bush. Turner had been quite friendly.

Walter wanted above all things to win the men round. He wanted to prove to himself that he could . . . but some-times he felt utterly miserable. His old place didn't fit him now. His old companions didn't want him. He found himself thinking of his brother officers with whom he had lived and fought. They had accepted him as one of them-selves ; he had never felt he wasn't wanted. What a fine crowd they were ! He would have died for any of them and they for him . . . some of them had died. He thought of the mess, the easy chat, the friendliness, the jokes. He thought of Jerry Mason standing with his feet apart holding forth about some utterly absurd idea, urging every one to fall in with some utterly absurd suggestion. He thought of John Paterson and Mark Sayers. What would he give to be back there amongst them, a friend amongst friends? What would he not give?

What am I? said Walter to himself in despair. Neither fish nor flesh.

This conclusion was a little ungrateful, perhaps, in view of the fact that he had been accepted as one of themselves by his brother officers in the regiment. But that was over now, the war was over, and Walter had deliberately given up that world and deliberately returned to the world into which he had been born, only to find that it did not want him. He had no friends at all in Old Quinings—with the exception of Kate Hardy. It was an important exception, of course, but although he valued her friendship highly he sometimes felt it would have been better if he had never met her. Oh, Kate, said Walter to himself, gazing with unseeing eyes at the landscape which a moment ago he had been admiring with so much pleasure, oh, Kate, it *would* have been better for me if I had never met you. . . .

Walter reared his ladder and fixed it against one of the beams which supported the roof of the barn, running across the building from side to side high above his head. Great thick oak beams, they were, made of the same material as the wooden walls of Old England. This barn had been built in those days—the days of wooden ships. How solid it was! Walter admired the workmanship which had gone to the making of it. Fine wood and honest work, the sort of work and materials that stood the test of time. He climbed the ladder nimbly, and peered into the dim recesses of the roof. Seager was right; there was junk stored away up here, pieces of sacking stuffed into corners—harbouring dirt and mildew. It must all be cleared away before they could examine the roof properly. The job was awkward. It would have been a good deal easier if he had had help, but he wasn't going to ask Mr. Seager for another man to help him —that was very certain.

Several hours passed. Walter pulled out the sacking

and threw it down. He worked methodically from one end
of the barn to the other. By midday it was done, the roof
was clear, and it was time to knock off for dinner. He had
brought his dinner with him—as he always did—and had
left it beside his jacket near the door of the barn. It was a
meat-pie to-day (Walter needed that meat-pie ; he was
hungry and his mother's meat-pies were delectable, juicy
and savoury with crisp light pastry which melted in the
mouth).

Where did I leave the ladder ? thought Walter, sitting
astride a beam and looking round. The ladder was gone
. . . no, not gone, exactly ; it had been taken down and was
lying on the floor. Beside it, sitting on a pile of hay, were
the four men—Reuben Doubleday, Turner, Curtis and
Robinson—they were sitting, eating their dinners in complete silence. Walter had not heard a sound ; he had been
busy working, of course, but they must have come in very
quietly.

" Hi ! " said Walter cheerfully. " I want to come
down."

" Come down then," said Doubleday.

" Nobody's preventing you," added Curtis.

" Joke's over," said Walter, still quite cheerfully. " I
want my dinner if you don't mind."

Doubleday laughed. He waved his hand and said
in mincing accents, " Send up his lordship's dinner
immediately."

The other men sniggered. Turner looked a trifle uncomfortable but Turner was a coward. There was no help
to be had from Turner.

Walter hesita.ed. He could take a joke as well as anybody, but this was not a joke. Reuben had done it to make
him look a fool—and had succeeded. Walter felt an absolute
fool perched up on the beam. He knew that this was doing
him no good with the other men ; it was making his position
with them worse than before, it was undermining their
respect. Hitherto if they did not like him they had at least
respected him, but Walter knew they would never respect

him again if he began to plead with Reuben to let him
down. Plead with Reuben ! He'd see him damned first !
Walter's anger rose, he was tired and hungry, and the sight
of the four men sitting there eating their dinners with an
elaborate show of enjoyment was the last straw.

There was an old piece of rope hanging from a beam
on the other side of the barn ; it was thin rope such as is
used for baling hay, and was probably rotten into the
bargain, but Walter was too angry to weigh the risk. He
rose and ran along the beam, grasped the rope and swung
himself over. The rope held until he was half-way down,
and then frayed and broke. . . .

Fortunately Walter knew how to fall. (He had practised
in Burma. It was a useful accomplishment there ; quite
often one had to climb into the top branches of a jungle
giant to view the landscape and plan one's future movements.) Walter fell, he rolled over and over, and jumped to
his feet.

" Now ! " cried Walter in furious tones. " Who moved
that ladder ? If he's a man let him stand up and say
so."

Reuben stood up. He said, " So you want your face
pushed in ! I've been ready to do it for weeks, Major
Walter Stack." He took off his jacket, folded it carefully
and placed it on the floor.

This was not the first time Reuben and Walter had
fought ; they had enjoyed many a good bout in the days
before the war. Reuben was heavier than Walter, he had
always been heavier, and he had unusually long arms which
gave him a definite advantage. In the old days Reuben
had nearly always won, and it was obvious by his attitude
that he had no qualms as to who would win to-day in this,
their first unfriendly fight. Walter was seeing red. The
whole history of the last few weeks was rising in his mind,
every insult he had endured, every unfriendly look con-
tributed to his rage. This was the culminating point. As
he stood there waiting for Reuben to take off his jacket he
remembered Reuben's strength and his long reach—but he

was too angry to care. Reuben might win, but not easily ; Walter intended to give a good account of himself.

At this moment there was a flash of lightning and a roll of thunder, and the rain began, but neither Reuben nor Walter noticed it.

" I'm ready," said Reuben. He stepped in, feinted with his right and aimed a hook with his left. Walter moved his head and avoided it.

The fight was on . . . but it wasn't going to be much of a fight. Walter realised in the first twenty seconds that he had Reuben cold. Reuben had deteriorated ; he had been drinking—not hard, but steadily over a period of months— there was no weight behind those punches and his reactions were slow. Walter, toughened by his years of service, his senses sharpened by the necessity for rapid decisions, had the big man at his mercy. Quite suddenly all the anger left Walter and he was sick of the whole thing. What on earth were they doing, fighting like this, he and Reuben ? He was filled with disgust at the chain of events which had brought them to this pass. He decided to end it quickly ; that was the best thing to do.

Walter feinted and launched a smart blow—not a very hard one—intended to tap his opponent's claret and end the fight, but Reuben moved his head and it got him on the mouth. He reeled backwards into a pile of hay.

The fight had lasted barely two minutes and very little harm had been done, but Reuben had had enough. He sat up and wiped his mouth—his lip was bleeding.

" You bastard ! " cried Reuben. " It was a foul blow, that's what it was, but I'll be even with you yet."

" It was a perfectly fair fight, and you know it," declared Walter. " You're soft, that's what's the matter with you."

" A foul blow," cried Curtis. " I saw it with my own eyes."

" Unprovoked assault," exclaimed Robinson. " You took him unawares. You couldn't beat Reuben in a fair fight. You never could."

Walter stood and looked at them—so they were solid, were they ? They were banded together against him. The knowledge that they hated him so profoundly made him feel sick. They would say this about him—all of them—and he would have to go. They had found this way of getting rid of him. He saw in a flash what it would mean : the disgrace of it—a man who didn't fight fair—the disgrace not only to himself but to all he stood for, all he had tried to stand for : the disgrace to his rank, the disgrace to the Service to which he owed so much.

" Turner ! " cried Walter, looking at him. " Turner, you saw what happened ! "

" I didn't see nothing," mumbled Turner with a shame-faced air.

" But I did," said a cool, clear voice from the doorway. " I saw the whole thing."

CHAPTER TWENTY-FOUR

FIVE HEADS turned with one accord towards the doorway. The speaker was Kate Hardy. She stood there, leaning against the doorpost. Outside, the rain was falling in a curtain of silver—there were raindrops in Kate's hair. She was pale and her eyes were very bright, her bosom was heaving.

" I saw the whole thing," she repeated, and she looked up to the beam in the roof.

There was a little silence. Nobody spoke or moved.

" Come, Walter," said Kate. " You want a piece of plaster for your hand."

Walter looked at his hand in surprise. He had not known it was bleeding. He picked up his jacket and followed Kate down the hill. They crossed the stepping-stones and went up through the garden in the rain—Kate leading and not looking back. (The garden was glorying in the rain, the flowers were full of crystal drops, there was a chorus of bird song from the trees.) They went through the house and into the kitchen. Walter sat down on a chair.

"Let me see it," said Kate. "Oh, Walter! And it's so dirty! You must have a wet dressing on that."

"It's nothing," replied Walter. "A good wash and a piece of plaster is all I want. Don't bother about it."

Kate took no notice. She put on the kettle and fetched lint and oil-silk. Walter watched her as she made her preparations, He was surprised at this new side of Kate, this capable serious side. She knew what she was doing and did it without fuss.

"Where's Martha?" he inquired.

"They're all out," Kate told him. "Milly had to go back to town, so Martha went with her to help her to clean the flat, and Susan is having lunch with her father. I rather enjoy having the house to myself."

She was ready now. Walter held out his hand.

"It's a horrid cut," declared Kate. "I suppose you knocked the man down. Was that what happened?"

"Was that what happened!" echoed Walter in amazement. "But you *saw* what happened, Kate!"

"Not—actually," she replied, looking at him with a doubtful sort of smile.

"Kate!"

"Oh, I know," said Kate, nodding. "It was—it *was* a lie, of course, but I had to say something, hadn't I? It seemed the best thing to say."

"But you looked up at the beam!"

Kate did not understand. She said, "I looked up because they were all staring at me and I couldn't look them in the face. I hate telling lies, really."

"When did you arrive on the scene?"

"Just then. Just that very minute. I heard you ask that man if he had seen what happened and he seemed unwilling to play up. You looked a bit worried, so I thought I had better take a hand. You see, I was in the field when the rain started and I ran like a hare for shelter in the barn—I thought they would notice that I was panting after running up the hill. Walter, honestly I hate lies, but sometimes they are necessary—besides, I only said I saw the whole thing. I didn't say what I'd seen, did I ? All I said was *I saw the whole thing*."

" It was marvellously effective," said Walter. He began to laugh. He laughed until the tears ran down his cheeks.

" Don't, Walter," said Kate, laying a hand on his shoulder.

" It's so funny," said Walter, trying to control himself. " It's so damned funny, isn't it ? For seven years I've been thinking about this place and longing with all my soul to get home, and now this ! How they hate me ! "

" It's jealousy, that's all. It isn't worth worrying about. *They* aren't worth worrying about."

" I'm not worrying about them."

" You are, Walter. You're trying to win them round because you won't admit that they have the power to drive you away. They aren't worth it, honestly."

" I can't go on now," said Walter in a dull flat voice. " It's finished. It wouldn't be fair to Mr. Seager. I'm a failure. I thought I could do it. I thought at least I could make mother happy, but I can't do that either."

" You'll get a job somewhere else—easily—a more suitable job. You're wearing yourself out, you're miserable here. It will be far better somewhere else."

" I know," said Walter desperately. " I know all that . . . but I don't want to go away . . . from you."

" Take me with you," said Kate quietly.

" Kate ! "

" Oh, Walter, don't be so blind. . . ."

" Blind ? "

" Yes, blind. Blind and stubborn . . . I'm doing this so badly, but I've never proposed to any one before ! " cried Kate, half laughing, half serious.

" Kate, listen——"

" No, I won't listen," cried Kate.

They were both standing now. Kate put her hands on

his shoulders and looked up into his face. Walter put his arms round her and kissed her.

It was a thoroughly satisfactory kiss. Kate had been kissed before, but never like this ; she had never imagined a kiss could be so dynamic.

" There ! " said Walter. " What about Stephen now ? What about Francis Drake ? "

" You're jealous of them ! "

" Yes."

" But they're you, Walter. They're both you. I believe you knew that all the time."

" I thought perhaps we were both Stephen——"

" Do you want me to give up Stephen ? " asked Kate, smiling into his eyes.

" I don't want you to give up anything," Walter said. " I can't . . . I mean, what are we to do ? "

" Get married, of course."

" Oh, Kate ! Would it be a success ? "

" We love each other."

" But is it enough ? There are all sorts of things to be considered——"

" Don't let's consider them, Walter. Don't let's consider anything or any one except ourselves."

" We must," declared Walter.

" You're afraid ! "

" Yes, desperately afraid. If I failed in this——"

" How could you fail ? We know and understand one another. We aren't children."

" Kate, listen to me. You're successful, well-known, wealthy ; you have dozens of friends——"

" None of that matters."

" It does," said Walter earnestly. " It does matter. All sorts of things would crop up and that feeling of knowing and understanding would be swamped."

" You feel that we know and understand one another ? "

" Yes, of course," he replied. " Of course I feel it. I felt it the first time we met. But supposing it didn't last ? Supposing we . . . lost each other. . . ."

" It's nonsense, Walter," she cried. " How could we lose each other ? "

He was silent.

" It *is* nonsense," she repeated in a quieter voice, " but —well, we'll talk it over if that's what you want. Let's go into the morning-room, shall we ? "

They went into the morning-room and shut the door.

" Walter," began Kate. " I don't see why——"

" We mustn't rush into this," interrupted Walter. " Kate, you do understand, don't you ? It isn't because I don't love you, it's because I love you so much. It's so tremendously important, it's so new——"

" New ? " she asked. " Do you mean you never thought of it before ? "

" Never," replied Walter. " I loved you, of course. I think I've always loved you, but I never thought of marriage. I thought you and Mr. Morven——"

" Oh, goodness ! " exclaimed Kate. " Every one seems to have decided——"

" Then it wasn't true ? "

" No, no, no. Does that satisfy you ? "

" But, Kate——"

" I am aware," interrupted Kate. " I am *fully* aware that every one in Old Quinings is of the opinion it would be a suitable match—provided his wife divorces him, of course—but strangely enough I have my own ideas on the subject ; and it seems to me," continued Kate with some heat, " it seems to me that, after what has happened between us, you might have realised that the rumour was false."

Walter saw she was annoyed, but he wanted the whole thing cleared up. " Why does he want a divorce ? " asked Walter in a low voice.

" That's his business, isn't it ? Perhaps he wants an heir."

She was really angry now, her eyes were blazing, and Walter was bound to admit to himself that her anger was justified. She had offered to marry him and he had raised this ridiculous argument about Mr. Morven—it was unpardonable, it was an insult, he must have been mad.

"Well?" demanded Kate. "Well, what about it, Walter? Have you considered the matter? Do you think it my duty to provide the Morven estate with an heir?"

"Oh, Kate!" he cried. "I know you think I'm a cowardly fool—and perhaps I am—but we mustn't——" He stopped.

There was the sound of footsteps on the gravel and a moment later Richard Morven appeared at the open window.

Kate was taken aback; she was completely dumbfounded (for she had just been speaking of Richard, and not very kindly). Walter was equally at a loss. They stared at the newcomer in silence, and if Richard had not been so full of his own affairs he must have noticed their discomfort.

"May I come in?" asked Richard, stepping in without waiting for a reply. "You aren't too busy, are you, Kate? I brought Susan back safely; she's run round to the kitchen."

Kate managed to say she was not busy, not in the least.

"Hallo, Walter!" continued Richard. "How are you getting on? Settling down into the old groove?"

It was very kindly meant, and kindly said, but could anything have been worse, thought Kate with a pang of dismay. Richard was not clever about people, he was not instinctive. He was set in his ways and thoughts.

They were talking now. Walter, standing up and looking very soldierly, was deferring to Richard as an older man, but not deferring as a man. In fact, thought Kate, he was talking to Richard as he would have talked to his colonel; it was exactly their relationship in civil life.

"Yes, sir," Walter was saying. "Yes, I should like to come up some evening and tell you about it. We had some interesting experiences. I can tell you one or two things that haven't been broadcast—yet." He laughed, and Richard laughed too, but not very heartily. Richard was gazing at Walter in surprise.

Having settled the matter, Richard sat down, for he

had come to talk to Kate and had no intention of going
away until he had achieved this object. His attitude showed
quite clearly that he expected Walter to go. Walter looked
at him doubtfully and went.

In a way Walter was not sorry their conversation had
been interrupted by the arrival of Mr. Morven. It gave
him time to think. It gave him time to arrange his ideas,
which were in the most appalling tangle. Walter went up
to the moor and sat down with his back to the rock in the
exact spot where he and Kate had met on Sunday. To-day
was quite different. It was dull and overcast, the clouds
were low. It was not actually raining now, but thunder
still rolled in the distance with a sound which reminded
Walter of guns. The moor looked different, too. It looked
wild and unfriendly beneath the lowering skies.

So much had happened to Walter, one thing after
another, that he felt completely dazed. He had suffered so
many emotions in the course of a few hours (and he had
had no dinner, but he had forgotten about that). He had
come up here to think, but it was not easy to think seriously,
for he kept on remembering Kate's face as she had looked
up at him and said, " Don't let's consider anything or any
one except ourselves." But we must, thought Walter,
taking his head in his hands. We *must* think of other
people.

If he and Kate could live alone upon a desert island all
would be well, for there was real companionship between
them. It was rather wonderful when you thought about it ;
he and Kate were complete entities—here they touched.
Just here the two circles touched. You had the feeling that
nobody had ever understood before. Did this mean that
at last you had met the person you had been looking for ?
Did it mean you would go on understanding more and
more ? Walter thought it did—unless other things cropped
up and spoilt it. Yes, that was the trouble . . . other things,
other people. There were Kate's relations to be considered,
Kate's friends. Mr. Morven, for instance. Walter had read
Mr. Morven's thoughts quite easily . . . Walter Stack, the

son of his gatekeeper; Walter, who was sent for to put a
new staple on the garage door . . . a nice fellow, but hadn't
he got just a little uppish? That D.S.O., of course . . . a
pity it had gone to the fellow's head!

Walter laughed grimly. Mr. Morven alone didn't
matter, but he wasn't alone. Dozens of other people would
think the same thoughts and Walter would see them thinking them. Dozens of people would say to each other, "He's
done pretty well for himself, hasn't he?" and would deplore
the fact that Kate Hardy had thrown herself away . . .
"Must have been mad, of course," they would add, shaking
their heads or smiling.

Walter's world would be just as difficult and uncomfortable for Kate; more so, perhaps. There was Bertie, for
instance; Bertie, the black sheep of the family; the rolling
stone who had to be rescued at intervals from the consequences of his own folly; Bertie, who had never done an
honest day's work in his life! When Bertie heard that
Walter had married a rich wife he would sit back comfortably and expect to be supported . . . it would be a sort
of blackmail, thought Walter wretchedly. His imagination
boggled at the mere idea of a meeting between Bertie and
Kate. Then there was his mother, of course. He had
promised his mother to come home and live with her and
his promise was sacred. Walter could not believe that any
project which entailed the breaking of that promise could
succeed. If he married a girl of his own class his mother
could live with them (it was often done and indeed it would
be the natural thing), but not with Kate—no, it wouldn't
work. It wouldn't be fair to either of them; he saw that
clearly. They liked one another, of course, but no, it just
wouldn't work.

The fact was Walter loved Kate too dearly to accept
what she offered; there was caution in his nature (and it
had been fostered by his training), caution and common
sense. In addition, Walter had lost confidence in himself
and his own powers; he had failed in his attempt to regain
his old place—what if he failed in this attempt? What if

he married Kate and saw love dying, killed by the hundred and one little details which were bound to come between them in everyday married life. I can't risk it, whispered Walter to himself. I would risk my own happiness but I can't risk yours . . . Oh, Kate, darling, it would have been better if we had never met !

CHAPTER TWENTY-FIVE

"HE'S A NICE young fellow," said Richard when Walter had gone. " He's changed a lot, of course. . . ."

" Isn't it natural that he should have changed ? " asked Kate rather tartly.

" I suppose it is," agreed Richard in a thoughtful voice. " In a way it seems rather a pity. A man like that may find it a bit difficult to settle down. Walter would find life easier if he had remained as he was—in his proper place."

" Easier ! " cried Kate. " Who wants an easy life ! Isn't it better to grow even if you have to endure growing pains ? "

Richard was a little startled at her vehemence. " Perhaps you're right," he said, but it was politeness, not conviction, which prompted the words.

He was silent for a few moments and then he said, " I like my daughter immensely."

" So you should," replied Kate. " Susan is a darling ; she's full of character and pluck. She's been horribly mismanaged, of course, but that's not her fault. Richard, we mustn't let Susan go back to her mother ; it's the worst sort of life for the child. Those doctors or psychiatrists—or whatever they are—have picked her to pieces and put her together again all wrong. It's a wonder she isn't a nervous wreck. If it goes on she'll be absolutely ruined."

" That's exactly what I came to see you about. I want to keep Susan."

" Oh, Richard, I'm glad ! "

He looked at her smilingly. " I'm glad you're glad, Kate. I thought you might be. Susan is absolutely devoted to you, so it seemed reasonable to suppose the feeling was mutual. I want my daughter—she's a Morven—her proper place is with me."

Kate nodded.

" I shall have to get rid of the Haygarths," continued Richard. " They do me quite well, but they wouldn't be suitable companions for a child. However, we needn't consider that at present. The great thing is you approve of my plan—that settles it, of course."

Kate hesitated, weighing her words. " You mustn't depend on me, Richard," she told him. " I can't promise to help you with Susan because I may not be here."

" Not here ! " he cried in alarm. " But I thought you liked the place ! "

" I do, immensely. The fact is—there is a possibility— I may be married."

Richard looked at her, speechless with consternation.

" It isn't settled," continued Kate in a low hurried tone. " Nothing is settled. I only told you because it seemed unfair not to—I mean if you're depending on me to help you. If you want me to—to keep an eye on Susan and— and that sort of thing. If I'm here I will—of course I will —but I may not be here."

" I see," said Richard in a dull flat voice. " Yes, I see . . ."

" I would have told you before but I didn't know. I mean the idea is—is quite new," added Kate.

" I see," said Richard again. He rose to go.

" Richard," said Kate earnestly, " you won't let this make any difference—about Susan, I mean. She would be happy with. you ; I know she would. There would be no difficulty in getting a governess or somebody. Anne Carlyle would help you."

" Yes," agreed Richard. " I won't let her go back. I promise you."

He was at the door now. He looked at Kate. It was

obvious that he wanted to know more ; he was wondering who the man could be—the man she intended to marry— it was natural that he should want to know ; but Kate had told him her news in such a way that it was impossible for him to ask.

"Good-bye," said Richard, taking her hand in his. "I haven't said I hope you'll be very happy. I do hope so with all my heart. The best fellow in the world wouldn't be good enough for you, my dear."

She watched him walk away, his shoulders sagging a little as if he were carrying a heavy load. She could not see him very well, for her eyes were full of tears. Why have we got to hurt people, thought Kate . . . people we like so much.

Susan and Kate had tea together. The child was full of all she had seen and done at the Manor and of all she intended to do.

"I shall live here with you," declared Susan in her usual determined way. "Then I can go and see my daddy whenever I like. Perhaps when I'm grown up I'll go and live with him and do the housekeeping. That would be a good plan, wouldn't it, Aunt Kate ? "

Kate listened to Susan's plans with one ear. She was thinking of Walter and wondering when he would come back. Walter had gone without a word, without a look which might have reassured her. He would think about the whole thing and then he would come back and tell her his conclusions—but what would they be ? She tried to remember all he had said, but this did not comfort her, for he had said nothing that gave her any hope. He loved her, of course, she knew that ; but she also knew that if Walter made up his mind that their marriage would be a mistake, nothing she could say or do would move him. She had seen how obstinate he was. In a way she admired his obstinacy—it was part of his nature and she would not have changed him. A man should be strong, he should know his own mind, he should do what he thinks right.

Kate had no doubts at all as to the right course. She loved Walter ; he was everything she asked for in a man. She felt him reach through her to something inside herself which until now had never been touched. This " something " was herself. It was what she meant when she said " I ". It was her inmost being. Nobody had ever got there before, nobody had ever aroused in her that feeling of spiritual kinship. Surely Walter must feel this, too. Surely he would come back and tell her that it was all right, that he loved her and nothing else mattered.

The evening wore on. Susan and Kate had supper together and at eight o'clock Susan went to bed. Walter did not come.

Kate went and sat in the morning-room and waited, but she had lost hope. If it had been good news Walter would have come before this ; he would have come and told her that it was all right, that he loved her, that they must be together always, that nothing should keep them apart. . . . So it was over, thought Kate. It was all over. Her romance had begun and ended with that one amazing and utterly satisfying kiss.

It was ten o'clock and Kate was still sitting in the morning-room with an open book on her knee when Martha came home.

" I'm back," said Martha, going forward to the open window and shutting it and pulling the curtains across. " I got the flat tidied up a bit for them—my goodness, it was dirty ! London was dirty, too—and noisy ! I felt quite dazed with the noise. It's a wonder to me how we ever bore it all those years. How did you get on, Miss Kate ? "

" Not too badly."

" Has Susan been good ? "

" Very good indeed."

" She's improving," declared Martha. " She's getting more reasonable. I don't mind telling you I'll miss that child when she goes away. She's good company, is Susan. . . . So you had a nice quiet day ? "

Kate did not answer that. It was difficult to answer.

"You're not feeling ill, or anything?" demanded Martha in sudden anxiety.

"No," said Kate. "No, I'm quite all right, Martha."

"You're sure? You're looking a wee bit peaky, Miss Kate."

"Just tired," said Kate with a sigh.

"You've been overdoing it," grumbled Martha. "That's what's the matter with you. I thought we'd have a quiet sort of time in the country, but there's a deal more going on in Old Quinings than there ever was in town—people coming and going and badgering you from morning to night, wanting you to do this and that and the other. You never get a moment to yourself in this place."

"But I like it," replied Kate, trying to smile. "It's interesting, Martha. It's life."

"If you like it, that's all right. I like it myself, to be honest. I wouldn't mind spending the rest of my life in the Dower House. It suits me down to the ground."

"We'll spend the rest of our lives here together," said Kate as she rose to go to bed.

Martha nodded. "Just you and me, Miss Kate."

"Just you and me," agreed Kate gravely.

The next morning was fine and dry. The garden looked particularly beautiful after the rain. The roses were in their second bloom, filling the air with fragrance. Kate had the french window wide open as she sat at her desk; her thoughts kept straying from her work, and her eyes were more often on the sunlit garden than the paper which lay before her. Every now and then she pulled herself together and struggled on, trying to fix her thoughts upon her story and bring it to a satisfactory conclusion. It was nearly finished now, she had come to the last few pages— she might finish the book to-day if only she could give her mind to it.

Suddenly Kate heard the sound of running footsteps on the drive. Someone was coming—someone who was in a hurry. It was Walter, of course. She knew it was Walter.

Kate waited with her eyes fixed upon the open window; her heart was bumping against her ribs, she could scarcely breathe. Walter had taken all night to think about it. In a few moments she would know which way the pendulum had swung. . . .

He was there, framed in the open doorway with his hands against the sides. "You're still here all right," he said, panting a little from his exertions.

"Still here?" asked Kate in surprise.

"Yes," said Walter, smiling. "I ran like mad because all of a sudden I was afraid you might have gone."

"Gone?" echoed Kate.

"That's what I felt," he explained. "I suppose it was silly but that's what I felt."

Kate did not understand. "Is it all right?" she asked in a dazed voice.

"It's all right if you'll forgive me," Walter replied. "If you'll forgive me for being a coward and a fool, and for insulting you unpardonably . . ."

"Oh, Walter!" cried Kate, rising and holding out her hands.

"But there's just one thing," said Walter, drawing back a little. "There's just one thing. I can't marry you without warning you about Bertie."

"Bertie!" exclaimed Kate. "Your mother told me about Bertie ages ago. Poor Bertie, don't let's worry about him. Don't let's cross our bridges until we come to them."

"It's a risk," declared Walter, hesitating.

"Who cares for risks!" exclaimed Kate, with shining eyes.

Walter came in and took her in his arms. She clung to him. He was tremendously strong and safe.

"Oh, Walter!" she murmured. "I thought I had lost you. I was sure I had lost you when you didn't come back. I can hardly believe this is true—it is true, isn't it?"

"It's marvellously true," he replied, holding her close.

They were silent for a few moments—perhaps longer. Time seemed to stand still.

" Tell me about it," said Kate at last. " What did you do ? Why didn't you come back last night ? I waited for you. Why didn't you come ? I was miserable."

" I was miserable too," he replied. " Utterly miserable."

They sat down on the sofa side by side, and he began to tell her what had happened. " I went up to the moor," he said. " I wanted to think, I wanted to try and get the tangles straight. It all seemed too difficult, it seemed hopeless. I was still wretched when I went to bed, still doubtful and worried. One moment I would think of you and decide that I couldn't possibly go on living without you, and the next moment I would see all the difficulties. Needless to say, I never slept a wink, and I felt like death when I got up this morning. Mother noticed, of course. She was bound to notice there was something wrong because I couldn't eat any breakfast, which is unusual to say the least of it. She stood and looked at me. ' Out with it, Walter,' she said. It was what she used to say in the old days when I got into scrapes," added Walter, smiling.

" I shall remember that," declared Kate. " I shall find it useful, no doubt . . . so you told her everything ? "

" Everything. It was quite easy because she understood ; in fact, I rather gathered she knew most of it already. She showed no signs of surprise and she never said a word until I had finished, then she said, ' Walter, my boy, you'll be a fool if you don't marry her. You'll never get anybody better.' "

Kate burst out laughing.

" Gosh ! " cried Walter boyishly. " Gosh, wasn't it rich ! I was absolutely speechless. It hit me in the solar plexus—it was a knock-out blow."

" What did you expect from her ? " asked Kate between her paroxysms of mirth.

" That was the joke," he replied. " I expected her to say, ' Walter, my boy, look before you leap.' "

" Go on," Kate adjured him. " What happened after that ? "

" When I recovered a little from the shock I found

myself feeling a good deal better. The knock-out blow had cleared my head ; I began to realise what an almighty fool I had been." He hesitated. Later he would tell Kate all that his mother had said ; how she had shown him that he was thinking too much of himself, not trusting Kate as he should. " You should trust her, Walter," Mrs. Stack had said. " She's chosen you and she knows what she's doing. She's no fool. A woman wants a man and you're a man— every inch of you. You go back and tell her you'll marry her to-morrow if she wants." Yes, some day he would tell Kate all that had passed between himself and his mother —but not now, not just at this moment.

" Mother had an answer for everything," continued Walter. " For everything except Bertie ; she agreed that he was a snag. Except for that one thing she had a plain solid answer to all my doubts. She was so sane—so sensible."

Kate nodded. " Your mother is the most sensible woman I know."

" Yes," agreed Walter. " Well, I've given my notice to Mr. Seager. He was very decent and said I could go at once if I liked. So I'm a free man . . . and the next thing to do is to find another job. You spoke of Sir Adam Bancroft ; do you really think he would take me ? "

" I'm certain of it," Kate said.

Walter rose and walked over to the fireplace and stood there for a few moments without speaking. He looked thoughtful, but he also looked confident and happy. He had the air of confident assurance which Kate had seen in him that first night. He had lost it, but it had come back. Kate was very glad.

" Kate," said Walter, " I told mother that we both wanted her to come and live with us. Was that right ? "

" Perfectly right," replied Kate without a moment's hesitation. " You promised to make a home for her and of course you must keep your promise ; besides, it would be lovely to have her. I'm very fond of your mother, you know that."

" Yes," nodded Walter. " I know—but mother won't.

She intends to live with Mary and Jack. She's quite, quite certain that she wants to do that. She seems to have discussed it with Mary. . . ."

"Well ? " asked Kate, watching him and waiting.

"So then I said she must come to us for long visits." He paused and began to laugh.

"And then," said Kate, smiling. "Then your mother said, ' I'll come when my first grandchild is born. You can't depend on nurses nowadays—*careless*, that's what they are.' "

"Oh, Kate ! " cried Walter, throwing back his head and laughing uproariously. "Oh, Kate, that's exactly what she said."

THE END